I0576013

RIGHTEOUS TRASH

BOOK 3 IN THE JAKE HALLIGAN SERIES

NICK KOLAKOWSKI

Rock and a Hard Place Press

RIGHTEOUS TRASH
by Nick Kolakowski
Copyright © and ™ 2025

Edited by Paul J. Garth and Roger Nokes
Cover by Heather Garth

ISBN: 979-8-9991000-7-8 (Paperback)
ISBN: 979-8-9991000-8-5 (eBook)

10 9 8 7 6 5 4 3 2

Published by Rock and a Hard Place Press, an imprint of Rock and a Hard Place Press, LLC,
Woodbridge, NJ.
rockandahardplacemag.com
amazon.com/~/e/B08WPQG5YV

Printed in the United States of America

PRAISE FOR
RIGHTEOUS TRASH

"It's odd, but in his own way, Nick Kolakowski writes relationship novels. That his books are filled with blood and guts and antic action can make you forget this, but always at the core of his books is a strong central relationship you care about, and that relationship is handled seriously. He does this better than ever in **Righteous Trash**, where the thorny relationship between a brother and sister is explored with depth, and, dare I say, earnestness. That he does this while telling a twisty tale that starts fast and never loses momentum is a tribute to his substantial talent."
— Scott Adlerberg, author of *The Screaming Child*

"A propulsive tale of violence and mayhem as two siblings fight for their survival within a criminal underworld. Nick Kolakowski writes with brutal confidence, depicting an America where the only currency greater than money is the power that comes from a gun."
— John Woods, author of *Lady Chevy*

DEDICATION

To DW.

PART 1:
THE RETURN

1.

It was midnight but I was still wide awake in bed when the security lights in the back yard blazed to life. That wasn't unusual: a stray dog or cat or runaway hog from the neighboring farm set off the sensors on a weekly basis. I lay there blinking, wondering if I should take the opportunity to get up and piss, maybe pop a painkiller to quiet the faint ache in my legs and ribs. My old war wounds liked to speak up whenever I went horizontal for too long, but that was okay—at my age, those scars and fractures were more like old friends than ghosts.

A few seconds later came the muffled rasp of metal from outside, and sad to say, that wasn't unusual, either: every so often, a meth head or other freak would lurk at the edges of the property, trying to find anything to steal or snort. I rolled from beneath the covers. On the far side of the bed, my wife Janine grunted softly and stirred, and I placed a comforting hand on her hip before slipping into the hallway.

Downstairs, I unlocked my gun safe and pulled a Glock 19 from my collection. In the past few years, Janine and I had survived a home invasion and a kidnapping, which had only solidified my desire to keep buying guns. If I wanted, I could have taken the AR-15 or the Benelli M3 or even the grenade

Frankie had gifted me one Christmas, but I wanted to evaluate any threats before I turned my property into World War III. I'd feel bad if I vaporized a cat.

I opened the back door a crack and paused to listen to the night. The security lights had clicked off, plunging the world into darkness again. As my eyes adjusted, I scanned for any movement in the little boneyard I'd started beyond the ditch that marked the back yard's rear edge. So far, it was stocked with three of my family's rustiest junkers, including the Toyota Camry I'd driven in high school and my dad's ancient Bronco. It wasn't out of the question that a desperate thief, having spied the cars from the road, was doing his best to saw out the catalytic converters.

I slipped through the doorway onto our porch, angling toward the steps that led to the driveway. From there, I planned on flanking the boneyard, placing me behind anyone lurking there. I had the Glock in a two-handed grip, my trigger finger resting along the slide, and I could sight and fire in a fraction of a second if someone was stupid enough to try anything. It might be a dumb teenager looking to score a few bucks in auto parts, but teenagers carried guns—

A voice from the black: "Bro. Chill out."

I paused, my pistol wavering. Confusion and excitement and fear all collided in my head like a set of out-of-control trucks in a snowstorm. "Frankie?" I called.

"You have any other sisters I don't know about?" That metallic scraping again, followed by the security lights flaring bright. Frankie stood in the dry weeds beyond the Camry, a short shovel in her left hand. She was dressed in a short-sleeved black shirt and a pair of dirt-smeared shorts, a silver pistol in a holster on her left hip.

"The hell," I said, lowering my weapon. After taking a bullet to the side a few years ago, Frankie had opted for self-exile in Mexico. The last I'd heard, she had a small house outside of Veracruz, where she ran freelance security for some local cigar factories and liquor distilleries. She also refused to let me visit, which offended me for a few months until I realized she needed time to soothe her enormous ego: the infamous Frankie Halligan, the most feared and whispered-about gunrunner west of the Mississippi, brought low by a .22-caliber bullet fired by a rich prick.

I'd spent all these years wanting to tell her it was okay, some of the bravest and most skilled men I'd ever known were killed by IEDs or 12-year-olds who squeezed off a lucky shot. No matter how good you are, your luck always runs out. But she wasn't the kind of person who'd absorb that lesson with grace.

Frankie stabbed the shovel into the earth beside her. "Sorry, I would have called, but you know how it goes," she said, and shrugged. "Operational security and all that."

"Did you put another bucket in my yard?" I asked, crossing the yard toward her. In her old life, Frankie had a habit of filling buckets and waterproof boxes with supplies and burying them across Idaho. One of those caches had saved our lives in the not-so-distant past, but I'd warned her about planting weapons anywhere close to where my kid played.

"Technically, it's not in your yard, more like your junk pile," she said. "Second, I'd have been a lot quieter if you hadn't parked this old hunk of shit right on top of it."

"How many?" I asked.

She sighed. "That one we dug up back in the day, remember, with the false IDs in it? Then this one. Then another on the other side of the driveway, which isn't even your property, I don't think."

"What's in this one?"

"You know, it's nice to see you, too. It's been too long."

I paused on the far side of the Camry, studying her in the fierce burn of the security lights. She had lost weight, her cheekbones sharp and shadowy, but that wasn't the worst part: her eyes were black holes, like her face was a mask and I could see the night through it. Something inside her was missing. It broke my heart.

The back door of the house opened, framing Janine in silhouette. "What's going on?" she called.

"Hey," Frankie said, waving to her. "Just digging shit up in the dead of night."

From across the yard, I could sense Janine's irritation baking off her like heat. Frankie had always churned up the waters of our marriage: Janine understood I couldn't abandon family, but she didn't like the idea of family selling guns and shooting people—and she'd never wavered on that point, even when Frankie saved her life a few times.

"We're happy to see you," I told Frankie, and meant it. Ever since she'd left, I'd startled a little whenever my phone buzzed or the doorbell rang, expecting bad news from down south.

"What brings you around?" Janine called, as casual as if Frankie had driven up to the house on a typical Friday night.

"I decided to open a new chapter in my life," Frankie said. "Should we be talking quieter? I don't want to wake up my darling niece."

"She's with my parents," Janine said. "Coming back in a week."

"Too bad." Frankie shrugged. "But maybe for the best. I know it's confusing, me showing up like this. Thank you for the hospitality."

Janine shrugged. "Sure." Then she turned and went inside, slamming the door behind her.

"It's okay," I said. "She just doesn't like being woken up in the middle of the night."

"Who does?" Frankie pried the shovel loose and rammed it into the earth again. "You asked what was in here. For starters, a bit of cash wrapped in plastic, along with a couple of phones that are probably dead. I need that cash to make a lot more cash."

"Why?" For a stupid moment, I thought she might mention credit card debt or a mortgage, the same everyday things that had snared me, but that wasn't Frankie.

"Because I'm staging a comeback," she said. "Gonna be bigger than ever. And while we're at it, we got some past sins to wash away, too. You'll love it."

I'd never admit this to Janine, but I'd always rooted for my sister, even when she was leaving heads in duffel bags. There was just one thing that bothered me. "What past sins?" I asked.

"Too complicated to explain late at night with a shovel in my hand," she said. "But trust me, you'll be involved."

"Are we killing people?"

"Only if they decide to be assholes." She offered me a wolf's smile. "In the meantime, we have some money to earn. I'm going to win Crazy Bill's Shooting Contest."

2.

Crazy Bill's Shooting Contest was legendary among firearms aficionados. Crazy Bill was the heir to a huge agricultural fortune who'd used his money to buy 500 acres of crap land near Lake Lowell, west of Boise. On two acres of that land, he built a tactical range littered with barrels, shot-up mannequins, and pop-up targets. Where the property's edge abutted an abandoned gravel quarry, he set up a 900-yard rifle range with stationary and moving targets. If you've participated in either pistol or rifle competitions, you know that neither of those setups are unusual—but Crazy Bill gave his contest some twists that lived up to his nickname.

At the start of the contest, every participant needed to complete the tactical range, where they were graded on speed and accuracy, before immediately moving to the rifle range for a series of long-range shots. This mix of short-range and distance shooting screwed those contestants who were effective with a pistol but clumsier with rifles, not to mention those who could blast the balls off a fly at half a kilometer but couldn't hit a moving target with a 9mm from five feet away. Plus, the rifle range was swept by fierce winds, and Crazy Bill let the grasses grow tall enough to obscure some of the targets along the quarry's outer rim.

That mix of formats aside, Crazy Bill's setup wasn't particularly special. There are competitions in Montana and Wyoming that demand you shoot targets at 2,000 yards and beyond, where you'll lose if you're not a master in everything from mental focus to wind calling. I'd competed in a few of those, mostly shooting .300 PRC, but I never had a chance of winning—I saw them more as opportunities to hang out with my friends and drink beer.

On the pistol side of things, the West is littered with contests that demand you plug dozens of targets quicker than Doc Holliday, so Crazy Bill wasn't an innovator on that front, either.

No, Crazy Bill's Shooting Contest was a unique beast because the old coot loved pranks that threw you off your rhythm and destroyed your concentration. He might bury air horns around the quarry and set them off just as a contestant took aim at a target. He was known for triggering random explosions at minimum safe distance on the tactical range, startling gunslingers into missing easy shots. One year, he paid a friend with a helicopter to hover low over the rifle range so the downdraft would interfere with the ballistics.

It was insane.

It was totally unprofessional.

And yet people put up with it because Crazy Bill offered a crazy purse: one hundred thousand dollars in cash. He also allowed for side bets, which could mean a million dollars on the property on game day. The purists might have turned up their collective nose at Crazy Bill's antics, but every year he attracted a mix of marksmen, former JSOC boys, bros with expensive guns they could barely use, and squinty-eyed rednecks like me. Most were competent marksmen. All thought they had a shot, so to speak, at winning the big prize.

Then you had Frankie.

She had won Crazy Bill's Shooting Contest twice, using the money in both cases to help fund her gunrunning empire. It was a thing of beauty to watch her out on the course.

If she wanted to rebuild her life fast, she would need to win again.

3.

The afternoon after Frankie's unexpected arrival, Janine brought me a nonalcoholic beer as I fired up the grill on the back porch. One of our neighbors had gifted me with a pair of pork tenderloins in exchange for a little work on his truck engine, and I'd done up some chicken wings with a barbeque sauce of my own infernal design. My head was still reeling from Frankie's reappearance, my emotions veering between excitement and fear.

"I feel like I should have brought you something stronger," Janine said as I opened the grill to expose its flaming heart. The meat sizzled as I carefully draped it above the coals.

"Uh oh," I said as I popped open the beer one-handed. "What's up?"

"Homeowners insurance," she said. "Went up a lot."

"Bad?"

She crossed her arms over her chest, tapping her elbows with the tips of her fingers. It was a mindfulness routine that helped ease her OCD symptoms. "Yeah," she said. "I called them, and they said they couldn't help it, it's because of all the fires in the state. They didn't say 'climate change' but you could tell they were blaming that."

My anger flashed white-hot, like lightning, before flickering out. Even a passing mention of our bills set me off these days. "But we keep the area around the property clear," I said, and it sounded too much like I was pleading.

"I explained that, too. They said there was nothing they could do." She tapped her elbows harder, faster. "You ask me, they're just trying to squeeze out a profit."

"Of course they are. Bastards. How's it work with our budget?" I asked, already knowing the answer: it wouldn't. Janine's household-expenses spreadsheet was a sea of red and getting worse, thanks to the interest on loans. As a bounty hunter, I'd tracked down so many people who'd done stupid things for money—defrauded their relatives, shot their siblings, robbed gas stations for the buck-ninety in the register—but it wasn't until I was swimming in debt that I understood, on a gut level, the desperation that led them to pick up that gun or fake that check or steer head-on into another car.

"Can you pick up more hours?" Janine asked.

I shook my head. "I can ask, but it's not damn likely, Janine."

"Don't raise your voice at me." She stepped back. "It's not my fault."

I paused to take a sip of fake beer. Thanks to a miracle of science, it tasted a lot like the real thing, except now I missed the alcohol. Back when I drank a lot more, chugging four or five beers in a row would smooth out life's rougher edges without slowing me down. Why had I stopped? Alcohol was like nature's stress reliever. Why didn't I—

No, I couldn't think like that.

"It's not my fault," she said again.

How many times had Janine and I broke up and gotten back together over the years? Four, off the top of my head. We'd even gotten divorced and re-married. *The road of love is a bumpy one*, she'd once written to me on a Valentine's Day card. *But there's nobody I'd rather ride it with than you.* I'd always shared that feeling. Even at my worst, I meant well.

"Sorry," I said.

"It's okay," she said, moving closer to me again. "Where's Frankie?"

I jabbed a thumb toward the house. Frankie was upstairs, using our newly upgraded broadband and a VPN to do things I hoped weren't too nefarious, if only because I didn't want the cops kicking in my door. What had she meant about cleansing our past sins?

Janine shaded her eyes and scanned the fields tinted amber in the sun's dying light, the faint shimmer of the Snake River and the hazy ridgeline beyond that marked the Oregon border. "You talk to her more about why she's back?"

"She's been vague so far," I said, hoping Janine would leave it at that.

"What was in that bucket she dug up?"

"A couple of fake IDs and old phones, a hard drive," I said. "And some cash."

"Like a block of cash? Like thousands?"

"No, more like a slim roll." I raised my hand, my thumb and forefinger an inch apart. "A couple hundred bucks, maybe. Walking-around money."

"Too bad. I was thinking she could help us out. Since we're hosting her for however long."

"She needed all that money for something. It wasn't much." I placed a hand on her shoulder, hating how she tensed slightly. "We're going to get everything settled, okay? We always do. You talk to the kid?"

She relaxed and leaned into me, her warm cheek against my chest. "Yeah, she's having a great time. You knew they were going rafting in Stanley?"

Janine's parents had taken our adorable tyke on a two-week trip of Idaho in their tricked-out RV, showing her everything our great state had to offer. "Yeah. I told you about that part, remember?"

"No." She puffed her cheeks and blasted out air. "I don't want to think about it. She can swim, though. She's a good swimmer."

"They wore helmets and vests," I said. "And they didn't go down the scary route. But that's not what freaks me out."

"What freaks you out?"

I waggled my eyebrows. "We've gotta wean her off finger steaks once she's back."

"Great. I look forward to, like, five weeks of reprogramming her diet."

The back door creaked open. Frankie stepped onto the porch, blinking in the setting sun like a vampire rudely awakened from a nap. She had a phone in one hand and an opened beer in the other. "Hey," she said, squinting at Janine. "I'm not going to be a burden here."

"Okay." Janine squeezed my biceps as she peeled herself from my chest, turning to face Frankie with a tight-lipped smile. "Were you listening to us?"

"I didn't need to," Frankie said. "I can see it in your face."

"Why'd you come back, sis?" Janine asked. "Why now?"

Frankie flicked her gaze to me. "Mexico got a little tough. This is home. I figure I still have enough juice to start again. Does that help answer your question?"

"I don't know," Janine said. "How deep you plan on dragging my husband into it?"

The smoke from the grill stung my eyes. I stepped aside and opened the cover and flipped the meat, which wasn't remotely close to burning, maybe it wasn't even time to turn it, but I needed to draw their attention to me, defuse this conversation before it went Chernobyl. "Hey," I said, doing my best to keep my voice low and reasonable. "We've all been through a lot together. Way more than most people. And we all respect each other, yeah? We can say what's bothering us but just . . . keep that respect thing in mind."

"Thanks, Mister Rogers," Janine said, but her shoulders relaxed.

"Seriously," Frankie said, leaning against the porch table. "You sounded a little too much like a self-help manual there, bro."

Janine turned to Frankie.

"I'm sorry," Janine told Frankie. "I'm just stressed. We have a lot going on."

"I know." Frankie sipped her beer. "And I'm here to help, believe me. We have more than enough enemies out there."

I sipped my own zero-proof brew, wondering how bad things might get, because my sister was a steamroller, a thresher, whatever metaphor you wanted to use for people who tore through the world. I tried to chuckle, to lighten the mood still further, but my chest felt too tight. The house and the fields beyond shimmered in the heat blasting from the grill, as if this life I'd so carefully built was on the edge of melting.

4.

The next day, Frankie was helping me prepare for a controlled burn at the edge of my land. I had paid a few kids to cut firebreaks around a half-acre square of scrub and weeds, and I intended to char everything inside of it black before the Fourth of July, which was a month away. The locals liked to celebrate our fair nation's independence by setting off fireworks, and the last thing I needed was an uncontrolled fire sweeping through the drier brush all the way to my house. Imagine how much *that* would jack up my home insurance.

Before we could torch the land, I had to remove the last items from a rusty shipping container sitting on the parcel. The container had come with the house, and I used it to store spare parts and fertilizer, which we dragged outside in the stifling heat and dumped into the cargo carrier of my ATV. Frankie begged me to leave the fertilizer in the middle of the field—*supersize that blast*, she said—and while that might have been fun, I didn't want a mushroom cloud to bring fire trucks all the way from Oregon.

"I have a proposition," I told Frankie.

She paused to wipe her sweaty hands on her hips and pull her skull bandana from her nose and mouth. The dust in the container would clog your lungs unless you covered your airways. "Who are we killing?"

"Nothing like that." I lowered my own bandana so she could see my face, know that I was serious here. "I want to put money on you in the shooting contest."

"Sure. How much? A hundred bucks? Two hundred?"

"Uh, more like a hundred grand."

She snorted. "What?"

"I'm serious."

Her black eyes lasered into me. I shivered despite the heat. "You have a heart operation I didn't know about?" she asked. "A second family you got to support?"

I had to look away. "No. It was just . . . everything hit at once," I said. "My hours at the gun shop aren't great, the mortgage is a bitch, and don't get me started on some other stuff. So, I have a plan. I'm gonna borrow some cash."

"Who's going to give you a hundred grand, bro?"

"Ivan the Terrible," I said. "I was asked to bring him in years ago, and I didn't do it, and he knows that. I figured that might earn me a little easy credit."

The idea of approaching Ivan had popped into my mind the previous night. As I stared at my bedroom ceiling, I dismissed it as lunacy—until I tried thinking of other ways to raise a big chunk of cash quickly. Nobody would buy any of the land behind my house, accessible only by the road cutting though my property. I couldn't make enough off my spare cars or guns, especially once you factored in taxes.

No, I needed to make a big move.

I did the math: a hundred grand multiplied a couple times would solve all my problems for the rest of my life.

There was a lot of risk, but what choice did I have? Go big or die. I couldn't stop the chaos swallowing up the world beyond my front door, but a lot of money would help me keep it at bay forever.

Frankie whistled softly. "You didn't cuff him because he's way too heavy for some bounty hunter to handle, and you know I mean that literally and metaphorically. He always had a crush on me, too, make of that what you will. Too bad I have zero interest in dating a cliche."

"He'll give me the money."

"Sure, and take your liver if you don't repay him. Why put yourself in danger like that?"

"Because nobody else will." I swept an arm across the landscape, from my house with the mortgage pegged to a bad interest rate to the cars that always needed repairs to the small parcel of land to our left that I'd borrowed too much to buy. "I'm drowning. I made some mistakes. I'm going to put it on you, and you're going to win, because you're the biggest badass I know."

I spent almost a year in Baghdad as the city tore itself apart. The dry crack of distant rifle fire, punctuated by the dull boom of IEDs. Columns of black smoke curling into the smoggy air. It was chaos, everyone at each other's throats, and I was happy to come home to what I thought was relative peace. Except this country was splitting apart, too. Maybe my time as a bounty hunter had soured me to the human race, but it seemed like half the people around me were angry—murderously angry—and the other half were too high to trust. My home was my safe place, the eye of the storm, and I couldn't lose it.

"Did I mention I developed a tremor in Mexico?" Frankie said, snapping me from my thoughts.

"What?" I asked.

"A tremor." She raised her hand so I could see the fingers quaking slightly. "It's not bad, but it throws my aim off a few inches . . ."

"Why didn't you fucking tell me before?"

"Relax, I'm fucking with you." Her hand stilled. "I'm steady as a rock. But don't you fret, I'm gonna win that contest, because I need that money, too. But on the highly unlikely chance I don't? We'd need to kill Ivan and any of his goons that look at us funny. Because I refuse to lose you, even though you smell funny, and you still can't tell jokes. Can you live with that?"

"I guess I'll have to." I had Ivan's number via one of his lieutenants, a small-time pill dealer who'd spent years taking my money in exchange for information. "Just aim steady, okay?"

We drove the loaded-up ATV to the front of the house, where we muscled the fertilizer and equipment into the new shed I'd built beside the driveway. After that, we swung inside, not bothering to shed our shoes because Janine wasn't home to freak about tracked dirt. I fetched two nonalcoholic beers from the fridge, along with a lighter and a roll of paper towels. When we returned to the rear acreage, I torched the towel roll and walked along the firebreak, lighting patches of dry grass as I went.

The wind was sweeping hard from the east and the brush caught quickly. We adjusted our bandanas over our faces to block the rising cloud of ash and watched the flames chew the grass to glowing cinders. Many years ago, at the height of our worst troubles, Frankie had set a fire that burned many gunmen to death before they could murder us, and now, as I watched her silhouetted against the inferno, I wondered if she ever regretted the pain and destruction she'd left in her wake. Frankie liked to position herself as a psychopath—it was good for business if nothing else—but I knew she loved our family. Maybe that love allowed her to do the most terrible things.

At the far end of the square, the line of fire fizzled out in a final burst of pale smoke. We yanked down our sooty bandanas and popped open our beers and toasted each other. "Here's to you," I said.

"Is it even a proper toast if the beer doesn't have alcohol?"

"Yeah, because it's my property. I make the rules here."

"Good enough. Here's to not killing too many people." She tapped her can against mine, then drank.

I hesitated before sipping my beer. Not because I disagreed with the sentiment—I dearly wanted my killing days behind me—but because Frankie asking anything of the universe seemed like a jinx, a sure way to bring down hellfire upon us.

5.

The Polaris Club's wet sauna was the size of a walk-in closet, and when Ivan the Terrible settled his massive weight onto the bench across from me, he loomed like a mountain of sunburned flesh, his pointy head wreathed in steam. Back in the day, when I'd refused to cuff him despite the enormous price on his oversized scalp, he told me I'd earned a favor. Today I hoped to collect.

"A hundred grand is not a small amount of money, even in this day and age," he said, his voice still bearing the faint accent of whatever post-Soviet hellhole he'd crawled from decades ago—on some days, he claimed Moscow as his hometown, Kyiv on others. "Tell me why you need it."

"I got expenses," I said.

"Considering your family, that answer is not good enough," he said, shaking his head. Sweat spattered the hot wood like rain. "You could send the money to your sister, and she could use it in ways that make my business more complicated. So, please, tell me why."

"I'm underwater," I said. "Mortgage, expenses. I just need to buy myself time to get right again. But nobody will lend to me because it's a lot of cash and I make, like, thirty grand a year right now if I'm lucky and—"

"Enough. I believe you." He waved a hand for me to shut up, then sighed long and loud. "I realize this is probably an idiotic question, but have you ever had a financial advisor?"

I shook my head. Two minutes in this little box and the heat was already starting to get to me. It reminded me too much of my time in the desert, sweating beneath my body armor, but I understood Ivan's need to have business meetings where nobody could wear a wire.

"Good. Financial advisors, they're not always dedicated to their clients' interests. Their real goal is to sell you an annuity or whatever else their company wants." Ivan smiled, his shiny teeth like tombstones in the rain. "Not me. My interests are aligned with yours, Jake. You need my money. I want you to repay my money with a little bit of interest. And you are a serious guy, so I am not going to bullshit you: if you do not repay, you know the consequences are real."

"I know."

"Good. I tell you the following not to intimidate, but to inform. Last year, a guy like you—not a bounty hunter, but a former soldier—took a loan from me. Fifty grand, high interest. And he opted not to pay it back. He thought his skills would keep me at bay."

"Let me guess," I said. "You killed him?"

Ivan shrugged. "You can find out for yourself. And yes, you are different from that fool. You are a man of honor. And I owe you, as much as I hate to admit owing anyone. So here is my deal: I will not charge you my usual rate. Instead, you will owe me fifteen percent annually on the balance. Do you understand what I am giving you?"

I nodded, trying to suppress the gratitude sweeping through me like a warm wave. The APR on my credit cards was 24 percent. I didn't want to think about my mortgage or my wife's student loans or any of the other gremlins eating up every paycheck as soon as it hit my account. Go figure: one of Idaho's worst human beings was proving more merciful than the banks.

"Good." He spread his arms wide, palms out. "If you want the money, it is yours."

"I want it," I said. "I'll pay you back."

"Interest payments start next month. The balance is due at the end of this year." His enormous head tilted, his black eyes drilling into me. "It is a lot of money, and the time will come sooner than you think. Remember, I am no bank. I also take payments in blood."

"I know," I said.

"Yes, of course. You are here, after all." Ivan slapped a sweaty paw on the bench, and a secret door popped open on the panel beneath, revealing a bottle of vodka and a dozen shot glasses on a tray. He opened the bottle and poured two shots and handed me a glass, and I almost hesitated to take it. I'd done my best to reduce my drinking, and although I still had my bad nights, I'd managed to limit myself to a few beers over the past three months. But I couldn't offend this man, either.

I slugged the shot. It burned going down, and I leaned against the sauna's tiled wall as its fire sank into my guts.

"How is your sister?" Ivan asked.

"I haven't heard from her in a long time," I said. "She's still in Mexico, far as I know."

"I always had a thing for her. A woman who can shoot the wings off a fly at a hundred yards. A businesswoman feared like a man. Very powerful." He winked. "I could handle her."

She'd tear your head off and shit down your neck, I wanted to say. Instead, I saluted him with my empty glass and said, "I'll convey the message."

"When you hear from her again."

"Yes. Whenever that is."

"Perhaps it is best that she is not here," he said. "There is a new man, he has the ridiculous name of Deacon Dunn, he is the big arms dealer now. Taking his territory, killing many men. A real barbarian. I keep my dealings with him to a minimum, but he is . . . hungry."

"I know of him." That much was true. When I quit bounty hunting, I'd lost most of my ears on the street, but Deacon Dunn was enough of a player—and a killer—for me to hear whispers about him.

"Someone to avoid," Ivan said, and raised the bottle. "Another?"

I shook my head and stood on shaky knees. "I appreciate the hospitality, but I need to be going. How do I pick up the money?"

"I'll text you a username and password. It connects to AlphaMojo, a crypto exchange, do you know it?"

"No." I tried staying away from anything related to crypto, although I sometimes felt like I'd missed out on something big.

"When you sign in, you will see a hundred thousand dollars in a stablecoin pegged to the American dollar. AlphaMojo lets you convert the balance and transfer it to your bank account. The taxes for any transactions are on you, understood?" He must have read the confusion in my face because he laughed and slapped his thigh. "What did you think, someone would hand you a duffel bag full of cash? I am not some drug dealer working his corner. My operation is sophisticated."

"I've never done anything in crypto before."

"Welcome to the new world, then." He poured himself a fresh shot. "The account used to belong to someone else. Ask no questions about who. On the first of the month, you will receive a text with the expected interest payment, along with instructions about how to pay. All smooth and professional. I aspire to top customer service."

I stepped to the sauna door and placed my hand on its fat handle. Through the steamed glass, the club's pool churned with midday swimmers. A different world moving in its rhythms, one totally alien to me.

"Jake," Ivan said.

I turned.

"Here's my other favor to you." He raised his hands and wiggled his index fingers. "If you fail to pay me back, I will take these. You will never pull a trigger again. But better than a slow death, perhaps?" He chuckled, and it sounded like a rockslide hurtling down a mountain.

"You're all heart," I told him, and left as fast as I could.

6.

After my shot of vodka at the Polaris Club, I decided to wait an hour before I drove again, because the local cops had a nasty habit of lying in wait on the route home. A long time ago, one of those cops had tried to kill my family as part of a conspiracy run by a few of the most powerful men in the state. I'd never been arrested or charged with ending that man's life, but the police have a long memory, and I didn't want to give them even the slightest excuse to make my life hell.

I wandered through downtown Boise, trying to reconcile its new construction with the memories of my misspent youth. The town always had a bit of a funky side (*Those who can, move to Portland,* Frankie liked to joke, *and those who can't, open a record store on 11th Street*), but I could never get used to the million-dollar condos and luxury spas and Tesla charging stations at the edge of parking lots.

I stopped into a new bookstore on N 8th. I'd found more time for reading during the slow hours at Garden 'N Gun. In the used-books bin, I spied a dogeared copy of a Stephen Hunter novel I'd read during one of my deployments, and the tug of nostalgia was enough for me to plunk down five bucks for it.

"Never read this one," said the tattooed hipster who rung me up.

"It's fun," I told him. "I read it in Iraq. Curious if it holds up."

"Oh yeah?" He bagged the book. "What were you doing there?"

I figured he was eighteen or nineteen. I'd been only a little older during my first tour. "The war," I said, telling myself to be patient. God help him if he was fucking with me, though.

"Oh yeah, like Saddam and that." He handed the book over. "We read about that in school. Thank you for your service?"

"Thanks, it was a long time ago," I said, and left before my anger triggered me into doing something dumb. The kid didn't deserve whatever I would have dished out. Time grinds forward, crushing everything before it, turning all of us into spirits—I think Frankie told me that during one of her goth phases.

The drive home was a nightmare. Construction crews were adding a lane to a long section of I-84 near Caldwell, slowing traffic to a crawl. I was bumper-to-bumper with the new residents of the subdivisions springing up in Nampa and Meridian. On either side of the highway, old farmland had disappeared beneath a growing sprawl of condos, car dealerships, and warehouses. You could blame it all on the Californians who'd moved here for the politics and cheaper real estate, or the local politicians who'd spent the past ten years refusing to plan for growth, but the net result was cars moving slower than I could jog.

I was also nervous, my sweaty hands flexing on the wheel, and not just because I feared cops breathalyzing me before I made it home. Under ordinary circumstances, there were no secrets between me and Janine, my wife. Except I couldn't tell her about Ivan's loan—she would freak, and worse, blame herself for the debts we'd run up over the past few years.

The traffic thinned as I approached my exit. No sign of cops. I bumped onto local roads, past gas stations and faded storefronts with their 1950s signage and dusty windows. The pace was slower out here, and I liked it that way. The only sign of life at this time of day was the line of cars parked in front of the local strip joint where I'd taken down many a subject during my bounty-hunting days. I took a right onto a farm road, and it was just me and miles of hop fields until I turned into my driveway.

I'd bought this house for the isolation and the spectacular view of the Snake River. A few years later, I'd snatched up some of the neighboring acreage because I had insane dreams of creating more of a farm, growing my own crops, maybe raising some livestock. While I wasn't a doomsday prepper like so many of my neighbors—it was expensive to build a bunker beneath your house—I saw the value in producing my own food.

Things were falling apart out there, after all.

Half the time, the grocery store had no eggs. Bird flu, or supply chain issues, or tariffs—the reason always seemed to change.

I worried about my kid ever finding a good job, because artificial intelligence was taking away anything that paid well.

And don't even talk to me about the violence out there, the crap on social media, the poison in the air and soil.

Better to button up, control as much as I could. Except the costs on the homestead skyrocketed faster than I expected, and

I was no farmer, and nobody could give me good advice—not even YouTube. I cut my losses. The cows and corn were gone, but I was still paying off bills for slaughterhouses, fertilizer, fencing, and more. We live and learn, huh?

Well, I'd learned I wasn't any good as a homesteader.

I turned into my driveway. Frankie sat on my front steps, dressed in her customary black cargo pants and t-shirt and sunglasses, a beer can in her hand and a crushed empty at her feet. "How'd it go?" she called once I shut off the engine and climbed out.

I shrugged. "I got it."

"Good," she said. "You won't regret this."

"I hope so," I said, pausing to look over the house, which seemed so small against the broader sweep of the fields and river, a tiny white speck that might disappear in an instant.

7.

The day after my meeting with Ivan, we sat on the back porch as Frankie stripped, cleaned, and inspected the components of the Accuracy International AXSR rifle she planned on using in the tournament. As she used a leveling kit to prep her scope, I said, "That's a pretty nice setup."

"I met up with Monkey Man while you were in town," she said. "I didn't ask where he got it."

The Monkey Man had served as Frankie's chief lieutenant in her heyday as a gunrunner. I'd never seen his face, because he made a point of wearing a rubber monkey mask whenever he was out in public. Nobody ever questioned him on that fashion choice because he was crazy enough to blast people apart in broad daylight, but he had been loyal to Frankie, and that was good enough for me.

"How is he?" I asked, opening my battered laptop to connect with the house's Wi-Fi.

She shrugged. "He seemed a little off, but I've been away a long time. He said he's working on a freelance basis. I told him I was thinking of coming back, setting up a stake, and you know what he said?"

"That he'd help out?"

"Nah, he said I should stay retired. His exact words were, 'It's healthier that way.' I must be slipping because I didn't slap him for that."

"When he wasn't giving you questionable advice," I said, "he mention whether he broke in that barrel?"

"Duh." She rolled her eyes. "Fired it a hundred times, he said. Cleaned it every two-dozen rounds. It's fine. My shots are gonna stay supersonic for two thousand yards, which is ultimately all I give a shit about."

I logged into that AlphaMojo website with the username and password provided by Ivan. The account had the promised hundred grand in stablecoin. A handy FAQ in a drop menu explained how I could liquidate the stablecoin and transfer the resulting U.S. dollars to my bank account. I followed the directions, hesitating with my finger over the 'Sell' button. This was the point of no return.

"Bro?" Frankie asked. "Everything okay?"

"Sure," I said, and hit the button before I could reason myself out of it. My stomach flipped.

Frankie squinted at me. "Okay." She reached into the canvas bag on the seat beside her and drew a TTI Sand Viper, a showy 9mm pistol that I knew retailed for several thousand dollars—if you could find one. "Beautiful, huh?"

"Oh God," I said.

"What?"

"I knew you liked John Wick, but that's ridiculous."

"Well, for your clarification, dear brother, John Wick uses the Pit Viper in the fourth movie, which is an updated variation of the Sand Viper, and very much not the same gun. Don't question me on that one, I've seen those movies more times than you can count with your little brain." She pulled back the pistol's slide to verify an empty chamber. "But all that aside, this is a good gun. Smooth action, accurate. It'll be the best thing on the range."

I swallowed, my stomach settling. "Ivan mentioned a guy named Deacon Dunn."

She cocked her head, offering me the same kind of smile you'd give a scared child. "Is that what's got you worried?"

"A little. I've heard of him before. He's heavy."

"I'm heavy, bro. And yeah, he's taken some of the territory I vacated, and yeah, he's sent some people home in bags, but from what I've heard, he's just another punk." She racked the pistol's slide again. "But he's not the only thing bothering you."

"What you said earlier about past sins. I need you to tell me more."

"It would spoil the surprise."

"I'm serious. As you're aware, past sins have a way of biting us in the ass."

She sighed as she took the pistol apart and set the components on a clean cloth. "Okay, maybe keeping silent was a jerk move on my part . . ."

"The great Frankie admitting wrong. Oh my God."

"I was being a jerk because I was nervous, because I care about you, so shut up. I could explain, but maybe it's better if I show you. How do you feel about driving into Boise?"

"Given all the traffic, not great."

"I'll make it worth your while. We can stop at Fanci Freez, I'll get you that peanut butter milkshake you love so much because you're too much of an idiot to appreciate their floats."

"You're paying for my gas, too."

She rolled her eyes. "Fine. Let me finish cleaning this amazing gun first, though."

"You are bringing it with you?"

"Nah, it's too flashy for the street." She raised the edge of her t-shirt, revealing a belly band holster heavy with a Beretta. "This here's my daily driver."

While she put her rifle and showy pistol in my gun safe, I helped myself to another nonalcoholic beer from the fridge. I figured I would drive to my bank in two or three days and withdraw the money from the AlphaMojo transfer. I tried not to think about the size of this secret I was keeping from Janine. She was always big on honesty.

Hadn't I done my best to live above the board, paying my bills and the interest on those bills, checking all the right boxes? And what had it gotten me? Absolutely squat.

Maybe Frankie was right about being a criminal: if society couldn't treat anyone right, then why should anyone live by its rules?

That thought didn't make me feel any better.

When I stepped outside again, I felt like I was trapped in a car rumbling downhill without the benefit of brakes, my heart hammering against my sternum. After I left the military, a shrink had given me some breathing techniques for handling that feeling—breathe in for four seconds, hold for four, exhale for four—and they mostly helped. Not in this instance, though.

Frankie slipped through the door and closed it behind her, then turned to study my face. I was certain she could see through my forehead and read my spiraling thoughts.

"Bro," she said.

"What?" I replied, forcing my jaw to relax.

"Nothing." But she grasped my elbow, squeezed.

We drove into Boise, with me at the wheel because that's how we always rolled. The highway was blessedly quick in the middle of the afternoon, buoying my mood until I spotted the gray smoke smudging the horizon. A ridgeline was burning in the hills above town.

Frankie switched the radio to a heavy metal station that seemed determined to play all of Metallica's worst songs in a row. On any other day, I might have flicked it off, given her some grief over her music choices, but my irritation at the music drowned out my fears of the future, and for that I was grateful.

As we reached Boise, she had me drive to the North End, a ridgeline of quiet houses and thick trees just above downtown. A few houses proudly displayed rainbow and Black Lives Matter flags, which would have drawn odd looks at best in my part of the state. Frankie told me to park on the corner of Hill Road and 20th, in sight of a little brown house with a sharply slanted roof and a narrow yard dotted with yellow and red flowers. It was a cute place that twenty years ago I could have bought for a hundred grand at most, but now would cost eight times that, thanks to all the outsiders snatching up property.

"Good timing," Frankie said, pointing at the house. A teenage girl had appeared in the yard, her yellow linen dress stretched tightly over a hugely pregnant belly.

"Who's that?" I said.

Frankie squinted at me. "Yeah? You don't have any ideas? Any guesses?"

"No," I said. "But then, I don't hang out with many teenagers. Sis, what is this?"

The girl opened the mailbox at the head of the driveway and extracted an envelope. A blade of sunlight slanted through the trees and played over the small bones of her face, the icy blue eyes and mop of dry brown hair. There was something I recognized in those features, but the connection slipped away before I could grip it fully.

"Funny, I thought you would've been better with faces, considering the bounty hunting gig and all. It's Anthony's kid," Frankie said softly. "She's in deep shit, and we're going to help her. We owe him that much."

INTERLUDE:
NEW ORLEANS,
A LONG TIME AGO

1.

Seventeen years ago, long before I met Janine or became a bounty hunter, Frankie and I flew to New Orleans to attend the wedding of our childhood friend Anthony, who'd managed to snag a Southern belle from an absurdly rich family. We spent the day before the wedding with a bottle of whiskey on our hotel balcony, swapping stories about Iraq and gunrunning.

We had a two-bedroom suite at the Hotel Pierre, in the French Quarter, booked under one of Frankie's many aliases. It was a converted mansion, and every guest had access to its walled garden with a burbling fountain and gnarled trees that threw deep shadows across the gravel. Our rooms on the top floor, connected by a balcony with a wrought-iron railing, offered a bird's eye view of the rear. The balcony had two wicker chairs with thick cushions that felt heavenly after my cramped seat on the plane. This high up, a faint but steady breeze kept some of the sogginess at bay.

As we settled into the chairs, Frankie uncorked the whiskey we had bought at the corner store before checking in. She chugged the bottle while I stared at her with my eyebrows raised.

"Damn, sis," I said. "You gonna leave a drop or two for me?"

Frankie lowered the bottle and wiped her lips with the back of her hand before unleashing an epic belch. "Remember when we were kids, we'd do that soda-drinking contest, see who could burp the loudest?" She chuckled. "Dad's face would get all red."

"Served him right for taking us to that unlimited-refill place," I said, and snapped my fingers. "Hand that bad boy over."

She did, and I took a good slug. It was expensive whiskey and smooth going down. Although I had tried to limit my drinking since my last tour, it was a losing battle. Screw it, you only live once.

"Ever think about leaving Idaho?" I asked.

"You mean moving to a place like this?" she grinned. "I gotta tell you, some of those restaurants we passed on the way in, po' boy sandwiches with fried clams, along with a cold beer? If you kept those coming, I'd live in a booth in the back. The problem is . . ."

"The humidity," I said.

"Yeah. I can deal with heat, because, you know, we grew up in a desert and all. But this humidity, it's like trying to breathe through a towel." She shuddered. "Like being waterboarded. Then there's the whole hurricane thing. I wouldn't want to buy a house only for it to get flooded out."

When we'd checked in, the guy at the reception desk informed us the hotel had only recently re-opened after the hurricane three years before. On the drive from the airport, I was on the lookout for signs of devastation, but it was hard to tell whether the shuttered buildings and cracked streets were the aftermath of storm damage or just the casualties of a city wrestling with too many issues.

"It doesn't have to be New Orleans," I said. "But that doesn't mean you can't move somewhere else."

She squinted at me and snapped her fingers for the bottle back. "You getting sick of the wondrous land of Idaho?"

"I don't know," I said, returning the bottle. "When we were flying to Kuwait, you see a lot of things from the plane. It's a big world out there, and I feel like I haven't seen much of it. I love Idaho, but . . ."

"You can have both. Travel a bunch, then come back. It's good to have a home base."

"You're never leaving?"

"I do love Mexico." She sipped whiskey. "But it's not my place. I know how to hide down there, but not how to really live."

"You should take me down sometime. Show me some cool stuff."

"I'll take you to some restaurants that'll fry your tongue right off, the spice is so intense. In a good way, I mean."

We lapsed into comfortable silence. Beyond the garden wall, what sounded like a live band started up, drums pulsing the air, and I felt a pang of longing so intense it almost hurt. Imagine all the mysteries out there. Imagine all the things I'd never see.

I helped myself to a deeper pull from the bottle. "Here's how you can tell I'm from Idaho," I said. "I feel weird without a gun."

Frankie laughed. "I brought a gun."

"No, you didn't. You only did carry-on. How'd you get it past security?"

"Watch and learn." Standing, she disappeared through the balcony doors to her bedroom, returning with the package the hotel receptionist had given her downstairs. The labels were in Frankie's handwriting, and I guessed she had mailed it to the hotel before she flew north.

"You sent a gun to yourself?" My eyebrows shot up. "Isn't that mildly illegal?"

"Yes, it is," Frankie said. "I am also paranoid about random inspections, X-rays, all that good stuff. Which led to my patented out-of-the-box thinking."

Seated again, Frankie tore open the package and dumped a pile of foam peanuts into her lap. Sifting through the mess, she plucked out thick bits of white plastic, tiny black screws, and a cylinder pitted like a honeycomb. When the pieces snapped together, she had a cartoonishly oversized revolver, missing its hammer and firing pin.

"People say you can't 3D print a gun," Frankie said. "What they really mean is you can't 3D print a good gun. But I got a contact—don't ask who or where—who has a 3D printer that's next-generation stuff. Seriously, it's ten years ahead of anything else you can find on a shelf."

Placing the plastic revolver on her armrest, she reached into her pocket and extracted her rabbit's foot keychain. She unscrewed the keyring's brass cap and tipped the foot into her palm. Four .45 slugs spilled out.

After lining the slugs beside the revolver, she rifled through her clothing, extracting bits of plastic and metal from her pockets. Unbuckling her belt, she fiddled with the ornamental buckle until it popped open, revealing a steel bit that looked like a slim hammer and firing pin.

"You never cease to amaze me, sis," I said.

"I amaze myself," she said, clicking the final pieces into the revolver and loading it. "It'll probably crack apart after three shots. But I feel naked if I'm not carrying, you know?"

"Oh, I know."

"Want me to demonstrate my amazing skills?"

"Please, no."

Frankie cocked back the revolver's hammer and squinted down the barrel. "Please, yes."

I waved the bottle, swirling five dollars' worth of whiskey in the bottom. "It's not empty."

"Do it," Frankie said. "We're drinking for free tonight, anyway. Aim for that empty house on the other side of the wall. I don't want to plug anyone by accident."

I sighed and made a big show of rotating my shoulder, loosening the joints up. "Fine."

"And don't worry about cops. I was talking to some folks before we came down here, he said it takes twenty minutes for 911 to respond. Sometimes they don't come at all. And besides . . ."

Before she could finish her sentence, I tossed the bottle as hard as I could from a seated position, aiming for the crumbling wall at the edge of the garden. I wanted to catch Frankie off-guard, but she was too quick for me. Dipping the revolver slightly, she pulled the trigger. The bullet left the barrel with a metallic slap, and the bottle shattered into a cloud of glass and whiskey. Momentum and the moist wind carried the remains over the wall and into the overgrown yard beyond.

Someone in the hotel would hear. Maybe nobody would care. I had never been to New Orleans before, but I sensed its wild heart would overlook a lot, short of shooting a tourist.

Frankie scanned the revolver with an appraising eye. "No cracks. That's good. But this is a tool of the last resort." Returning the weapon to her armrest, she cracked her knuckles. "Before we get to the wedding, we're buying more alcohol. Being thoroughly sloshed is the only way to get through this wedding, wouldn't you agree?"

"Maybe we should keep a clear head," I said.

Frankie laughed and shook a finger at me. I'd always felt an overpowering love for my brilliant sister, even as she terrified me to my core.

2.

A hotel security man knocked on the door and asked if anyone heard a gunshot. By that point, Frankie was in the shower, leaving me to fake surprise as best I could. I even let him poke his head into the suite. After he left, I wandered into the living room that linked our bedrooms and turned on the widescreen television bolted to the wall.

I opted for the news. The lead story was a multiple murder in the Midwest, a group of Neo-Confederates gunned down outside their little clubhouse. Police had no idea who'd seceded them from existence. I turned the television off. As much as I always enjoyed a good example of the karmic scales balancing, I was sick of violence, which was too bad because I was good at it. I entered my own bathroom and changed into my off-the-rack suit, already dreading the hangover that surely awaited tomorrow morning.

When I returned to the living room, I found Frankie in a lacy black dress, wedding traditions be damned. "Still packing?" I asked.

She hefted a beaded black purse with a beaded gold strap. "You bet. Plus, I got a knife strapped to my leg. Anyone gets between me and the bar, I'm gonna stick them like a pig."

"That's the festive spirit," I said. "But you'll have to change clothes. You can't wear a black dress to a wedding, remember? Have you ever worn actual colors?"

"I will neuter you," she shot back.

"Oh, come on." I grinned at her, warming to my theme. "I could see you rocking some hot pink. Or maybe white?"

"Before we leave this city," she said, her voice rising to a feral scream, "I need to stop for another *drink*."

It was still too early for New Orleans to reveal its craziest side. Outside the hotel, a few bloated tourists stumbled down the street, clutching oversized cups. On the corner, a man in a wheelchair was tuning up a trumpet, a bucket beside him. The restaurant across the street had its windows open and I could hear, over the roar and boom of football on a half-dozen widescreens, a guitar ripping inexpertly into Lynyrd Skynyrd's most famous song.

I wasn't much of a partier—large crowds made me nervous—but I could see the appeal of a neon-gritty place like this. It didn't judge. It wanted to give you what you wanted, so long as you wanted liquor, drugs, gambling, a warm body for a few minutes or a night.

It was peak America, and I had fought in the sand for it, lost a few chunks of my flesh for it, suffered through nightmares for it. I'd better like it.

Frankie hailed us a cab. Twenty minutes later, a few blocks from the highway onramp, Frankie had us pull over so she could buy a bottle of beer. The driver, an older gentleman in a golf cap and a polo shirt, said, "Big night?"

"Wedding," Frankie said, and slapped a hand on my shoulder. "Not to each other. We're related."

"Doesn't stop folks sometimes." The cabbie chuckled. "You see all sorts of weird shit down here."

"I bet," I said.

"Next time you want to get smashed, heading to a big event? Ask your driver to take you to the daiquiri drive-through, okay? They give you this cup big as a missile, and they put a little piece of tape over the straw so it's still a closed container, technically." Our driver winked at us in the rearview mirror. "That way, no cop has a problem with you driving with a drink."

"We'll keep that in mind," Frankie said, twisting open her beer and draining half of it in one gulp.

We passed a row of wrecked houses, the windows black and broken as an old skull's eye sockets, the outer walls colorful with graffiti. "That's from the storm," the driver said, almost to himself. "Wish they'd knock it down. A blank lot's better than that."

"Maybe they will. Things change," Frankie said.

The driver snorted. "Yeah, things change. Soon the whole country will look like that."

He was killing our buzz. I tapped Frankie's arm as discretely as I could: be quiet. The driver flicked the radio to a slow blues station, and we sat in silence for the next thirty miles.

The venue was a classic plantation house in the middle of nowhere, three stories of white pillars and black balconies under an arched roof, fronted by a gravel driveway lined with torches on long wooden sticks. We had the driver leave us at the head of the driveway, to avoid the snarl of vehicles dropping off passengers at the front door. I noted the valets scrambling to park luxury SUVs and sports cars, their foreheads bright with sweat. With nightfall, the temperature had dipped a few degrees, but the air still felt thick as syrup.

"Wonderful," Frankie said, hurling her empty beer bottle into the swampy grass beyond the firelight. "Rich pricks. I guess they suffered no pain from Katrina, huh?"

"We knew what we were getting into," I said. "Anthony's done well. I should've been a lawyer."

"And what's the lovely bride do? Remind me." She slung her purse strap around her wrist. I wondered if the revolver inside would shatter the next time she pulled the trigger.

"Public relations, I think."

"Whatever that means." We had arrived at the front steps, where a large man in a tuxedo smiled and gestured for us to follow a torchlit path around the side of the house. It must have taken an army of workers and tens of thousands of dollars, but Anthony's parents had transformed the lawn behind the mansion into a glittery fantasia of lights and white tents.

"Stop being nervous," Frankie hissed.

"Sorry, too many rich bastards around," I said. "Can't help it."

"Don't worry, they don't bite." She almost stumbled off the path. "Not like we can, at least."

A dance floor with a checkerboard pattern, lit by guttering torches, dominated the lawn between the tents. On the bandstand beside it, a few musicians in red vests warmed up their instruments, and the empty seats around them suggested a full orchestra would soon appear. I grinned at my sister and asked, "Gonna wow everyone with your dance skills later?"

"Tough girls don't dance."

"Fine, you can stand back and admire my mad tango skills."

"Last time I saw you dance," she said, "I almost forced a belt between your teeth. I thought you were having a seizure, what with all the shaking and twitching and whatnot."

"I do my best. I'm in serious need of a beer." I nodded at the bar inside the nearest tent, where three bartenders poured drinks while a fourth used a pick to chip bits off an ice sculpture into glasses. The sculpture was shaped like an elephant with a downward-angled trunk. It steamed faintly in the night air.

"I'll come with you," Frankie said. "I plan on double-fisting, and you don't have enough hands to carry mine and yours."

"This is supposed to be a fancy party."

"I'm not a fancy lady," she said. "Come on."

We were halfway to the bar when the crowd parted, revealing the groom. As a teenager, Anthony's standard uniform had consisted of a t-shirt and jeans, usually stained with a combination of dried hot sauce, dirt, and chip crumbs. For his wedding, he had traded up for a white seersucker jacket and dress shirt, black bowtie, and navy-blue pants. With the costume change, something seemed to have been swapped in his character as well: he stood straighter, his gaze direct, his smile wide and white as he marched toward us.

"Thanks for making the journey," he said, his handshake crushing. His attention shifted to Frankie. "This was a wedding, shrub, not a funeral. It wouldn't hurt you to act happy for once."

Frankie offered him the world's most feral leer, her lips peeling back from her teeth, but only held it for a moment before softening into a warm smile. "Just for you, you big nerd," she said, throwing her arms wide. "Bring it in."

Anthony submitted to her crushing embrace. "What you been up to?" he asked her.

"A little bit of this and that." Frankie stepped away and shrugged. "You know."

"Yep, I do." Anthony turned to me. "What about you, Jake?"

"Back from overseas," I said. "And glad to be here."

"Thank you for your service." Anthony nodded. "Listen, can I talk to you both for a sec? Alone?"

We followed him across the lawn, beyond the flickering line of torches that marked the wedding's perimeter. Farther in the night lay the marshland, with all its miles of mud and brackish water and creatures with sharp teeth. You could walk into that brush and disappear forever.

"I have something to ask you," Anthony said, taking a deep breath. Here it comes, I thought. He wants the kind of favor that only a couple of hardboiled friends can provide: an enemy beaten, or a loan collected, or a stalker driven off.

Frankie placed a hand on our friend's arm. "Whatever it is, it's okay," she said. "We're here for you."

"That's right," I said, although I mistrusted the words coming out of my mouth. "Whatever you need, buddy. Just say the word."

"Oh, good," Anthony said. "That's a relief. I wanted to write something on the invitation, but Bonnie said it'd be better if I asked in person. Can you help at the front of the house?"

"Help?" I asked.

"I don't think anything bad will happen, so it's not like we need two bouncers." Anthony offered a nervous chuckle. The confident man we'd met on the lawn had disappeared again, replaced by an overgrown teenager in his dad's best outfit. "But just sort of, I don't know, keep an eye out, just in case? If you get bored, you could maybe help with the coats, parking cars?"

"You have valets," Frankie said, her voice almost a whisper. "We saw them when we came in."

"Yeah, but, um, maybe not enough." Anthony stared at his polished shoes. "We're on a bit of a budget."

Maybe they did things differently in the South, but where I came from, the best way to deal with awkward situations was head-on. "Buddy," I said. "We're your guests. We've known you since we were kids. And you're asking us to become employees?"

"Employees get paid," Frankie said. "And I didn't hear any cash being offered. Not that you can afford my per-hour."

"You get to attend," Anthony said, so low I almost missed it.

"What the hell is this?" I asked, my voice rising. "We fly here and . . ."

"Bonnie." Anthony raised a hand, palm out. "I pushed for you, but it was a tight guest list and she . . . well, she doesn't appreciate you the same way I do. That was the compromise. You could come, but she wants you . . . more in the background."

"This is some repugnant bullshit," Frankie said. "What's wrong with us?"

"Bonnie comes from a different kind of family," Anthony said. "They're deeply connected. Powerful friends in high places, all that shit. And they have some weird ideas about, um, class and stuff. Listen, I'm just along for the ride here. You're my friends. Really. I'm just trying to figure this out."

"No need," I said. "We're leaving." The urge to hit Anthony was so strong it made my head hurt.

"No," Frankie said. "We'll stay."

I turned to her. Frankie's face was a blank mask in the dim firelight, her eyes a pair of black holes. She had crossed her arms over her chest, hands resting lightly on her shoulders. With her dark dress blending into the night behind her, she looked like a spirit emerging from the afterworld in pieces.

"Oh, thank you." Anthony puffed out his cheeks and blew. "Truth be told, it's been hard on me. Wedding planning, man, it's a mess. Thanks for understanding."

"No problem," Frankie said, and smiled, her teeth flashing with reflected fire.

Before I could say anything, Frankie gripped my elbow and escorted me away from Anthony, offering him a cheery wave over her shoulder. Instead of heading toward the front of the house, where presumably we would "help" with parking cars and screening guests, she guided us left, where the lawn ended in an enormous greenhouse lit from within by eldritch light. The crowds disappeared. An insect snapped past my head, buzzing for blood.

"I'm not helping out with shit," Frankie said. "Where does he get off?"

"He always was a little weak," I said.

"Seriously, he wouldn't have made it through Calculus 101 if it wasn't for me." She snorted. "He's lucky I don't valet for him. I'll take one of those fancy cars and crash it right into a wall."

"We can leave," I said. "Go back to the hotel. It's New Orleans. It'll take us three minutes to find something socially unacceptable to do."

"Oh no," she said. "We're going to do something socially unacceptable right here. He thinks wedding planning is a mess. Let me loose."

Beyond the greenhouse, we found a brick garage with five doors, fronted by a wide gravel path that swooped around the side of the mansion, where presumably it connected with the driveway. Beside the garage stood an enormous cage of heavy-duty wire, filled with dark shapes that rose at our approach. A soft growl drifted across the humid air.

"Dobermans," Frankie said. "Excellent."

"Sis," I said. "Anthony might have it coming, but the guests don't."

"Let me work." Frankie stepped closer to the cage, the dogs snarling at her approach. "See, they have those thick collars. There's probably an invisible fence, stops them from running off the property."

I could feel her anger spiraling, a chain reaction that would end with someone dead. If I grabbed her by the elbow and dragged her toward the nearest alcohol, it might break that circuit, but maybe not. Frankie in a killing mood was more dangerous than a nuke with loose wires.

I was reaching for her when a man stepped from the shadows. He was older, his long sideburns gray, but his muscles strained against his tailored blue suit. He puffed a cigarette, its cherry casting a reddish glow into the deep valleys of his face. He had cop eyes that flicked over our faces and hands as we approached. "I hate weddings," he announced, blasting a lungful of smoke at a dive-bombing mosquito.

I shrugged. "Better than funerals."

"Depends on whose funeral," Frankie shot back.

"Where are my manners?" Tossing the cigarette at his feet, crushing it with his heel, he stuck out a hand. "Percy Avalon."

"Jake." We shook.

"Frankie." She took Percy's hand and squeezed as hard as she could. His eyebrows rising in surprise, he released her and backed away.

"Quite a grip," he said, reaching into his jacket for a crushed pack of American Spirits. "Want a smoke? I'm trying to get rid of these."

I waved a hand. "I'm okay, thanks."

"Sure," Frankie said. "You only live once."

"Nasty habit. I managed to quit for ten years." He extended the pack, letting Frankie pluck a cigarette free, before pulling out a fresh coffin-nail with his teeth. "Then work got tough. I couldn't take the stress. I'm weaker than I like to admit."

"I've gone through the same thing," Frankie said. "Just with killing people, not smoking."

Percy laughed. "You're funny. We can't be too hard on ourselves. Too much at stake." He torched Frankie's cigarette before lighting his own. "You two here for the bride or the groom?"

"Neither" Frankie said, blowing a smoke ring. "They're assholes."

I laughed a little too hard. "My sister and I, we're friends of Anthony from way back."

"Then you're from Idaho, I'm guessing."

Frankie snorted. "Got it in one."

Percy squinted at us through his smoke. "You don't strike me like friends of Anthony's."

"How's that?"

"You're not showing off, yelling about some piece of software you invented, like you want everyone to know what big balls you have. You're not prattling on about your cars or house or whatever."

"I just finished a tour in Iraq," I said. "I'm glad to be back."

"Thank you for your service," he said. "Frankie, what's your profession?"

"I'm an entrepreneur. I deal in hardware."

"What do you do?" I asked Percy, anxious to stop him from following up with a question about 'hardware,' because Frankie was angry and drunk enough to say something like, *I once vaporized a meth dealer with a .50-caliber machine gun.*

"I'm in private security. I was a New Orleans cop before that, but just for a few years," he said. "And the Marines before that, which was less crazy than being a cop here, if you can believe it. I'm only here because I'm friends with the bride's father. He called, begged me to show up. Said he needed the moral support."

The crunch of heels on grass, and a scowling bridesmaid appeared. "Ceremony is beginning in twenty minutes," she said. "You want to begin moving toward the seating area?"

"Do we have to?" Percy asked. It was a weak joke that made us giggle, nonetheless. The bridesmaid fixed us with a stare that could have set us on fire.

"We're coming," I said, waving her off.

She turned on her heel and stomped away.

"Maybe we can watch the wedding from afar," Frankie said.

"You're a hardass." Percy winked at her. "I hope your brother here won't be offended if I ask you to dance later."

I liked the idea: Frankie could afford to meet someone whose idea of a date wasn't firing off high-velocity rounds at a biker gang's clubhouse. "Doesn't bother me," I said. "But let's get through this thing, first."

The ceremony itself took place on a wide square of lawn beyond the tents. A pair of electric lights illuminated an elaborate altar wrapped in flowers and white beads, a crystal chandelier dangling from the crossbar. Two hundred people took their seats on folding chairs, and a priest with a reddened face and a headset microphone stepped before the altar. He offered some sage words on holy matrimony and the true meaning of love.

Beside me, Frankie made a drinking motion with her left hand, then rolled her eyes. I nodded: we should have grabbed something suitably high proof before taking our seats. Everyone around us had a glass in their hands, except for Percy, who had found a seat with the bride's family. I was starting to like the guy.

The priest wrapped up his speech. Beside him, Anthony trembled in his seersucker. He locked gazes with me, and I offered him my steeliest look in return. He swallowed and shifted to Frankie, who waggled her fingers. I felt her anger ratcheting down, and that was good: it's hard to keep a low profile when you've turned a rich couple's nuptials into a righteous rampage of revenge.

A pair of violinists struck up a jaunty tune, and Bonnie the Bride appeared: blonde, blue-eyed, her dress an elaborate tower of white lacy folds.

"She looks like a supermarket cake," Frankie muttered.

I elbowed her in the ribs.

The bride and groom said their vows, slipped on their rings, and floated up the aisle and across the lawn toward the big tent, the crowd drifting after them. I hoped we were at the same table as Percy, but no such luck: we found ourselves seated on the periphery with two other couples who ignored us. Dinner was macaroni with fancy cheese, paired with roasted pork ("The foods of our wonderful childhoods!" announced the small card beside our plates). Once the plates were cleared away, the musicians began to play, slow and low, and the guests migrated to the dance floor. Anthony, his bride, and their families lined up beside the bandstand.

Beside me, Frankie cracked her knuckles. "Hold my purse," she said, passing it to me before I could reply. I realized I'd been wrong before. She wasn't calming down; her anger had transformed from white-hot rage into a quiet, vicious thing.

One of the groomsmen stepped into the middle of the dance door, holding a wireless microphone. His face split into a wide grin and he pointed at Anthony, no doubt ready to dispense a witty story.

He never had the chance. Frankie appeared beside him, as if summoned by a dark spell, and snatched away the microphone. "Ah, Anthony," she said, working her voice into a cheerful boom. "How long have you been friends with me and my brother?"

"Since we were kids?" Anthony called. His face twitched, his eyes uncertain.

The groomsman stepped forward, hand extended for the microphone, and Frankie bared her teeth at him. "That's right," she said, pacing the dance floor. "We even went to college together. Anthony was an absolute beast at a keg stand, let me tell you. He could suck the chrome right off a trailer hitch. This one time, I offered him a dollar if he would jump off the roof of his frat into some bushes—and he was so drunk, he did it. Didn't break a bone because, hey, God looks after drunks and babies, am I right?"

Anthony chuckled but his smile was forced, his eyes frightened. Beside him, Bonnie's parents stared at their feet. Bonnie's cheeks flushed deep red, and the priest placed a wrinkled hand on her wrist, his face a lovely shade of purple.

"Anyway, it was college, so pretty much everyone was broke," Frankie continued. That was a lie. Other students might have survived those years on cheap beer and ninety-cent packages of dried noodles, but young Frankie sold guns to shady folks, earning enough to buy a ramshackle monstrosity of a house a few blocks from campus.

I suspected what Frankie was about to say, and it filled me with equal parts excitement and dread. Nobody would ever forget this wedding.

"But then our good buddy Anthony—we called him Ant—came up with a remarkable way to make some dough." Frankie paused for drama. "Our local sperm bank needed some . . . donations. I think fifty bucks a pop or something, provided you cleared the blood tests. That right, bro?"

Frankie jabbed a finger in my direction. I shrugged, offering the crowd a helpless smile.

"Yep, I do believe my brother also fired off a few rounds for fun and profit." Frankie's finger drifted until it settled on Anthony again. "And so did the handsome groom here. A lot of rounds, come to think of it. How many times you donate, Ant? A hundred? Two hundred? Did the clinic give you a frequent-flier award?"

The groomsman hissed a curse and charged across the dance floor, his jaw set, his eyes brimming with tears. Frankie studied his approach with a feral grin. "And I forgot to mention the best part," she said. "Anthony's idiot ass forgot to check that box on the forms that prevents your offspring from contacting you."

The groomsman closed in. He was so focused on Frankie's face that he forgot to keep an eye on her free hand, which had slipped beneath her dress. When he touched her wrist, meaning to twist the microphone from her grip, she slammed her foot onto his dress shoe, driving her high heel through the thin leather and his big toe. He opened his mouth to scream, and she pivoted behind him, neat as a tango dancer, squeezing his throat in a chokehold. Her free hand emerged with the blade she had clipped to her leg.

I elbowed my way to the edge of the dance floor, Frankie's purse-strap over my wrist, ready in case anyone tried to rush my sister from behind. I would crack the skull of anyone who touched her, but I had no intention of pulling out her plastic revolver. This wasn't a shooting affair. Not yet at least.

Frankie had the crowd frozen in place. Blade notched against the moaning groomsman's cheek, she purred into the microphone in her other hand: "Congrats, Anthony's parents: you have, like, three hundred grandchildren by this point. I know you're Catholic, and I heard that artificial insemination is a sin or something, but I bet you'll overlook that when they start showing up at Anthony's door. They'll be so cute. What do you think, Ant?"

Anthony had nothing to say, but the groomsman gurgled in Frankie's grip, his hands slapping at her elbow. "Hush," she cooed at him. "We're almost done here."

"Why are you doing this?" shouted someone in the crowd, sounding on the edge of tears.

"We get here, ready to celebrate Ant's wedding," Frankie snarled back, "and he wanted us to park cars. Is that any way to treat a guest? I mean, really."

Another guest barked harsh laughter.

"Anyway," Frankie said, and, removing the knife, planted her heel in the groomsman's backside and shoved. He tumbled to the floor, clutching his injured foot. "I know you might be tempted to call the police. Unless you want this wedding on the front page of the paper—for the wrong reasons—that's a bad idea."

"You should leave," someone shouted.

"Oh, we're gone," Frankie said, slipping the knife beneath her dress.

Beneath the bandstand's pale glow, Anthony and Bonnie looked like miserable zombies, and I felt a twinge of guilt. Had Frankie overreacted? Sure, it was an insult to ask a guest to work at your wedding, but Frankie had ensured Anthony would never have a comfortable conversation with his in-laws ever again. Those powerful, well-connected people who probably paid for his house and gave him a job somewhere.

Powerful, well-connected people who might not take kindly to a pair of rednecks embarrassing them at their daughter's wedding, come to think of it.

Oh shit.

I should have tried to stop Frankie, I thought.

But how do you stop a wolf like my sister?

"Clear a path," Frankie told the crowd, which parted, muttering, so we could leave the dance floor. We circuited the mansion and marched down the driveway without looking back. I figured we could head down the road a mile and call a car from there. A winged critter landed on my hand, nosing for my blood, and I smashed it flat. Once we left the protective ring of fires around the house, thousands of the little bastards would suck us dry. The perfect end for a perfect evening.

Gravel crunched. A black Porsche SUV crept along the driveway behind us. As it came alongside, the driver's window whispered down, revealing a grinning Percy. He had an unlit cigar clenched in his teeth.

"Hey, you crazy kids," he said. "You need a ride?"

3.

Frankie slipped into the front passenger seat while I flopped into the back. Percy had the air conditioning set to arctic chill, cooling the sweat that plastered my shirt to my chest. The cold felt marvelous, and I closed my eyes, dreaming of clean sheets, dark rooms, a world absent of alarms and phones. Despite the gallons of alcohol we'd consumed since afternoon, I felt only a little drunk.

As he maneuvered the Porsche onto the road, Percy fiddled with the radio until it landed on a classical station. We rode in silence, mosquitos flickering in our headlights. A clear drop spattered the windshield, followed by another.

"Is it raining?" Frankie asked.

Percy smiled.

I craned my head, sighting a yellow moon through the gnarled trees rising on both sides of the road. "Looks clear outside," I said, my words punctuated by three rapid-fire splats on the windshield.

"Yep," Percy said, flicking on his wipers. "You're definitely not from around here."

"You're freaking me out, man," Frankie said.

"It's bugs," he laughed. The wipers smeared the drops, leaving whitish streaks in the headlights' reflected glow. Pressing the button that activated the windshield washer, he added, "I used to own a convertible, and I tell you, I couldn't drive a mile at night in the summer without getting my daily ration of protein from the insects flying in my mouth."

"That's what you get for living in a bayou," I said. The SUV dipped into a low valley, the moonlight glimmering through the mist clinging to the trees.

"Ah, but I love it." Percy removed the cigar from his mouth, waving it around like a conductor's baton. "It feels like the edge of the world, in more ways than one. I know it's not, not really, but sometimes I'll get a big cup of coffee from Café du Monde—you absolutely must go there, if you haven't already, it's the one tourist trap that's worth it—and stand on the riverbank. There's this view of the bridge, and the lake beyond it, and the Gulf beyond *that*, and I always tell myself that I'm standing on the last bit of land before it all gives way to water. Like it's eternity out there."

"Sounds nice," Frankie said, her face turned to her window.

"It is. Good way to start the day, before the chaos really sets in. Because my life is chaos, let me tell you. I have this thing right now . . ." His voice trailed off, and he shook his head. "Never mind. It's boring."

"I really wrecked things back there, didn't I?" Frankie groaned.

"Yeah, you did," Percy said. "And you know what? You made it a memorable wedding. Every guest is going to dine out on that story for years, maybe decades. And sure, you pissed off

Bonnie's family, and your buddy Anthony isn't sending you a holiday card this year, but I bet they'll get over it. Just wait until they have the first kid."

"In Anthony's case, more like the two hundredth," I said.

Percy chuckled. "You're right. But you know, the first real grandkid, it brings a family together like nothing else. You have kids?"

"Not yet," I said.

"Never for me," Frankie said.

We veered from the local road to an onramp, the swamp giving way to a world of concrete and sodium lighting, the six-lane highway arcing us back toward civilization. Percy slammed the gas, and the Porsche hunkered down, eating the miles with a low rumble. I squeezed Frankie's shoulder, hoping she would put a hand on mine and squeeze back, but she remained as still as a statue.

"Bonnie's parents," I said. "Would you describe them as forgiving types?"

Percy shrugged. "You never met them?"

"No," Frankie said.

"They're sharks, I'll tell you that." Percy sighed. "They make enemies for a living, not that you'd know it to look at them. They're cordial, pleasant, like a bunch of people down here. 'Southern hospitality,' it just means they're smiling when they drive the knife in. Anyway, I've probably said too much. Keep it under your hat, okay?"

"Will do," I said, drawing my fingers across my lips like a phantom zipper.

A black SUV passed us on the left before swinging into our lane.

On our right, a white jeep matched our pace.

Frankie sat up a little straighter in her seat.

"Besides," Percy said. "I'm thinking of quitting. Just isn't for me. I have . . ."

The brake lights of the black SUV flashed as it dropped back, almost bumping the Porsche's front fender. Percy growled deep in his throat and edged the wheel to the left, about to change lanes. Beside him, Frankie clutched her seatbelt, her startled eyes finding mine in the rearview mirror a half-second before the white jeep swung hard into the Porsche's flank.

4.

I n Iraq, I lived in a constant state of hyper-alertness. Even on base, tucked behind concrete blast-walls and piles of sandbags and armed men on duty, I could never stop the trickle of adrenaline into my bloodstream. On patrol, kicking in doors and barging through houses, zip-tying wrists, sprinting across dusty alleyways as sniper bullets ate chunks of wall, my brain would twist open the chemical spigot, and the world would explode with color and noise and smell, everything on max.

It was terrible.

It was also addicting.

After I left the military and returned to Idaho, I would tell civilians that I never felt more alive than when I was under fire, and they would look at me funny. My brain had a hard time adjusting to that lack of things trying to kill me every day. I drove too fast. I drank too much, hoping against hope that enough beers and shots of whiskey would kill the dreams.

One night, I placed a cheap cigar close enough to my forearm to feel the heat, daring myself to jam the red-hot tip into my skin. You'll love the adrenaline, an inner demon told me. It'll take you back to Baghdad, just for a minute. My hairs crispened, and the smell reminded me too much of bodies burning in a Humvee. That night I dreamed of arms and heads flying through a cloudless blue sky. The next day I signed up for classes at the mixed martial-arts studio in the nearest strip mall, hoping for lots of sparring, trusting that a few punches given and received might finally sort out my traitorous head.

A part of me always missed combat mode.

When the white jeep plowed into Percy's Porsche, sending us airborne, my body straining against the seatbelt, I felt oddly at peace for the full second it took us to bounce onto the shoulder, a second that seemed to stretch into an eternity. I had time to miss my daughter and Janine. I had time to turn my head toward Frankie, her eyes wide with surprise. Beside her, dark blood spooled from a deep cut in Percy's head, his hands rising from the wheel like a Pentecostal visited by the Spirit.

We impacted—boom—the roof caving in, my skull exploding—

Black.

Pain in my hands.

Gravel and bits of glass sliding across my skin, my suit tearing in a dozen places.

Frankie gripped my shoulders as she pulled me through the shattered rear window of the Porsche, her feet braced against the frame for leverage. I shuffled my feet, helping her along, but my mind was a gray cloud crackling with thunderbolts of pain.

"What a fucking night," Frankie hissed.

Once my head and shoulders were free of the car, I had a better view of the highway. The black SUV and the white jeep had stopped a hundred yards away, their brake lights staining the air red.

Frankie yanked hard, pulling the rest of my body over the frame. She was tiny but mighty, my sister. Percy remained behind the wheel, crushed between his seat and the crumpled dashboard. Unmoving. Shadows cloaked his face. No way to tell if he was alive.

"Gotta get him," I mumbled.

"No time," Frankie said, trying to lift me. I shook off her hands and rolled over and rose to a crouch, then followed her off the gravel shoulder into the wilderness. When we reached the bottom of the incline, my feet sinking into the soft mud, I glanced back. Shadows flickered in the crimson gloom: men crossing the shoulder, leaping into the scrub. Someone shouted. They were trying to flank us.

We ran toward a dim line of scrubby trees, the muck sucking at our shoes. Frankie kicked off her heels, then reached under her dress and pulled out her knife. She handed it to me, then unzipped her purse and drew that ridiculous plastic gun. Once we slipped past the tree line, gnarled branches blocked the light from the road, reducing the world to a patchwork of shadow and the dank stench of swamp. Frankie gestured for me to stop running, and we crouched beside a rotting log.

We could have kept running, except I sensed an immensity of sludgy, lightless bayou stretching behind us. You couldn't move fast in mud up to your knees. If we were lucky, we might have made it a hundred yards in the open before they cut us down.

Who had sent these men?

Sure, we ruined the wedding, but that didn't mean the death penalty, did it? Even in Louisiana?

Adrenaline charged through my body. Despite the swamp's overpowering stink, I concentrated on my breathing, trying to steady it as best I could. Who the hell wanted us dead? Or were they after Percy?

A man approached the trees, his face a pockmarked moon, his stubby submachine gun aimed at the grass. I stood very still and waited for my sister to do something, because a knife almost never wins against a firearm.

The man stepped closer, squinting into the dark.

Frankie tossed her purse underhand to our left. It splashed.

The man swung toward the sound. As he did, Frankie stood and shot him in the head. Before his corpse hit the ground, Frankie slipped from the trees, firing again. To our left, another man clutched his chest and fell facedown. That second shot split her revolver's plastic barrel like a tree trunk hit by lightning, and she tossed it aside and sprinted toward the corpse of the first man, who still clutched his submachine gun.

Beside the black SUV, another man opened fire at us, bullets stitching a line of muddy spray. Frankie dove for the submachine gun, her black dress smeared with grime, and fired off a burst from a prone position. The shooter hit the pavement, his legs kicking.

"Thanks for the help," Frankie called as I emerged from the tree line.

Considering how much alcohol she had downed tonight, the fact that she could hit anything at all, much less a man at thirty yards in the dark, should have earned her an Olympic gold medal. "Seemed like you had it under control," I said. "Besides, you stuck me with the blade."

"Give it to me," she said, holding out a palm. "I'll need it if I got to cut Percy loose."

The black SUV roared away, leaving a cloud of scorched rubber. The jeep continued to idle in the left lane, its headlights bright.

"Here," I said, handing her the blade. "I'll find your stupid plastic gun."

She ascended partway up the shoulder and crouched and scanned for any additional threats. Just in case she needed backup, I looted the nearest corpse and found a Glock 19, fully loaded. After she disappeared behind the wreck of the Porsche, I figured she was safe, so I returned to hunting down her discarded revolver.

My sister might have insisted it was impossible to trace a 3D-printed gun, but I knew the cops were smarter than she liked to assume. I pulled out my phone and flipped it open, then used its light to scan the swamp around me. It only took a few seconds to spot the revolver's grip poking from the water.

I slipped the wet gun into my right pocket, its grip and hammer poking out.

Next, I needed to find her purse.

My light flickered over brown water, sharp grass, a rotting stump. I prayed the glow wouldn't attract an alligator hungry for a midnight snack, but that wasn't the only thing making me nervous. If we left any evidence behind, the cops could take us down for three, maybe four murders.

My light flashed off gold: the purse-chain. The purse lay at the bottom of a shallow puddle. After I retrieved it, I pulled out Frankie's phone and tried the power button. Miracle of miracles, the thing worked. I shook as much swamp as I could from the purse, but I doubted anything would remove that gassy smell from the fabric. Frankie was going to be pissed.

Purse in my left hand, Glock in the other, I ascended to the highway, where I met Frankie beside the wreck of the Porsche. "He's dead," she said, holding up a phone with a shattered screen. "I took this. Might say who took a shot at us."

"Great. And I got yours," I said, handing her purse over.

She unzipped the purse and dropped in Percy's phone. "You check those dead dudes?"

"Too busy getting your stuff," I said, gripped by a new fear: it was a small miracle that nobody had driven past, but our luck wouldn't hold forever. I spared a few seconds to examine the shooter dead in the middle of the highway. Kneeling beside him, I used my forearm to roll him onto his side, feeling his rear pockets with the back of my hand. He had a handkerchief, which I used to cover my fingers as I unzipped his nylon jacket and pulled out his wallet, which was empty except for eighty dollars in cash and a plastic card with a magnetic strip. The card was black, with no logos or numbers, and I slipped it into my pocket.

"We should leave," I said. "Whoever was in that SUV might come back."

"Sure," she said, using her phone to snap a photo of the dead man's face. "Let's take that jeep."

The collision with Percy's Porsche had crumpled the jeep's hood, but it handled well as I shifted into gear and drove off, Frankie in the passenger seat. After we put a mile between us and the corpses, I said, "What do you think?"

"Professionals," she said. "And I hope they were after Percy, because if not . . ."

"I haven't pissed off anyone lately," I said. "I mean, aside from tonight."

"Neither have I." She opened the glove compartment and searched inside. "Registration is for some guy named Dan Arnold. And that's the only thing in here, besides the owner's manual."

The next exit directed us toward New Orleans. I took it, my eyes flicking to the rearview mirror for any sign of the black SUV. Frankie twisted around in her seat, searching the back for anything useful. "This is fun," she said, retrieving a small plastic monkey. "You know what this means, right?"

"Professional killers like to carry kid's toys?"

She tossed the monkey at my shoulder. "It's not the only toy back there. Guys don't take the family jalopy on a kill mission, which means this car was stolen. Which means we need to dump it."

Did anyone at the wedding see us leave with Percy? Even if not, I bet that fabulous mansion had cameras monitoring the driveway. How long until the cops asked Anthony some questions? Until they put out an APB for our names and faces?

"We got to get our stories right," Frankie said, as if reading my mind. "In this instance, might not be the worst thing to tell a version of the truth. Percy crashed, we got scared and ran, hitched a ride back to town. Something like that."

The idea of a frightened Frankie was ludicrous. "What about all the bodies?"

"What about them? We left the scene. Got no idea why a bunch of randos decided to have a gunfight there right after."

"That's pretty half-assed."

"Remember, it's not what they suspect. It's what they can prove."

"Let's just get back to the city," I said, nodding to the faint lights of New Orleans in the distance, and thought about Percy back there in the humid night, trapped in his crushed-metal coffin. My hands squeezed the wheel until my knuckles popped white, but the gesture did nothing to stop my rampaging heartbeat. Unlike all those times in Iraq, I didn't feel more alive, just scared.

5.

Back in the French Quarter, I drove aimlessly, taking left after left after left, always on the lookout for a black SUV. After an hour, with gas running low, we abandoned the jeep near Louis Armstrong Park. I hoped someone with nefarious ideas would wander past, spot the unlocked doors and the keys in the ignition, and drive it to the nearest chop shop for speedy disassembly.

Before we walked back to the hotel, Frankie knelt on the sidewalk and smashed her plastic revolver to pieces and tossed the pieces in the nearest storm drain, along with my Glock 19. We took a roundabout route through the Quarter, staying away from the larger clusters of drunken tourists. My suit was a total loss, the jacket shredded, and Frankie's dress was spattered with dried mud and bits of grass. Nobody spared us a second glance.

"I never want to hear you talk shit about 3D printing ever again," Frankie told me. "It's experimental tech, sure, but it saved your ass."

"I could totally have taken out those guys with my bare hands. No problem."

"Oh yeah, absolutely." Frankie pointed at the nearest neon sign, which advertised BIG ASS BEERS. "Let's hit that bar. I need a drink. And food. I'm starving."

My stomach growled like an irate cat. "Hotel first," I said.

"Why?"

"Because we look like we just survived a gunfight in a swamp, that's why," I snapped. The drive had soothed some of my fears, but I was anxious over everything that might come next: cops, killers lurking in the dark, Anthony filing one hell of a lawsuit for emotional damages.

"Don't you dare get angry with me. I didn't ask for any of this crap."

That's debatable, I thought, thinking of Frankie's performance on the dance floor. "Sorry. Long night," I said, because I didn't want her to punch me in the face.

"Let's wash away our sins," she said, wiping at the streaks of drying mud on her cheeks. "Then we can figure out what to do next."

A block from the hotel, I stripped off my jacket and stuffed it under my arm. My shirt was wrinkled and a little stained, but nothing out of the ordinary for a wild night on the town. We crossed the lobby as fast as we could. The elevator was mercifully empty, and so was the hallway in front of our suite.

Back in my bedroom, I stripped off my suit and stuffed it in the trashcan. I would figure out how to dispose of it later. I took a two-minute shower, steaming hot, and changed into jeans and a t-shirt before returning to the living room, where I found my sister still in her wrecked dress, slugging back a small bottle of whiskey from the mini-bar.

"You realize each of those little bottles costs, like, ten bucks?" I said.

"Yeah, they're there to prey on the weak-willed and the soft-minded." Kneeling, Frankie freed the last three bottles of whiskey from the mini-bar's rack and lined them on the desk. "But you know what? I just survived a shootout, and I don't feel like going back out there quite yet, so we're just going to let the hotel win this one, okay?"

"We should think about checking out," I said. "Maybe even leaving the city. Whatever that was, I don't want it to become our fight."

"Sure," she said, cracking open a bottle and guzzling it down. "I checked Percy's phone while you were in the bathroom. Nothing on it, not even personal contacts. Who carries a burner to a wedding?"

I shrugged. "Doesn't matter to me. Whatever it is, it's *not* our fight."

"I'll send that photo I took of the dead guy to some contacts, but that's a snowball into Hell. I know, I know, it's not our fight, but you know what I really hate? People shooting at me. Really throws off my fucking evening."

"We should leave," I said. "I mean it."

"I think we have a little time before anyone kicks in our door," she said. "Meanwhile, brace yourself because I'm about to get philosophical."

"Oh no."

"Maybe even a little maudlin."

"Big word."

She snorted. "Come off it. You're the most well-read guy I know, emphasis on the word 'guy.' You like to pretend you're a redneck but you're nearly as smart as I am."

I popped a fresh paper cup loose from the stack on the desk and helped myself to a mini bottle of whiskey, not because I wanted the alcohol but because I didn't want Frankie even drunker on top of everything else we'd consumed today. When the adrenaline finally wore off, she'd have to contend with the world's worst hangover.

"What's making you philosophical?" I asked. "I mean, besides getting shot at."

"No, that's pretty much it," she said. "We got lucky. I've been lucky a long time. But someday, that luck's going to run out."

I nodded. "It usually does. The trick is to change things up, zig when fate thinks you're zagging. Maybe a profession where you get shot at a lot less."

"Said the soldier. So, what's your next move?"

"We check out. Get on the first plane out. Get back to Boise. Forget any of this ever happened."

She snorted. "No, dumbass, I meant in your life. Now that you're done soldiering."

"Oh." I shrugged. "No idea. For about two seconds, I thought about becoming a cop like Dad, but that doesn't feel right. Maybe security? Maybe something with guns, since I have all this knowledge."

"You could help me," she said, so quietly it was almost a whisper. "I can always use someone who knows guns."

No way, I wanted to tell her, but I also didn't want to hurt her feelings. As the daughter of a righteous cop, Frankie had grown up with a strong sense of right and wrong, bad, and good. *You can't add more evil to the world*, our Dad used to tell us at the dinner table. *No matter what.* I knew she got a perverse thrill out of breaking the law, but there was also the guilt, which is why she seemed determined to pickle her liver at every opportunity.

Except I didn't need to say the words when Frankie could read my silence. "One day, bro," she said, "you're going to realize you're more like me than you'd ever want to admit. You won't always be able to deny it."

"We'll see," I said. "But what about you? I don't want your luck to run out. When are you going to get out of running guns?"

She reached for the last bottle of whiskey, and I snatched it away, snapped it open, and downed it as she squawked in protest. "No fair," she said.

My throat burned and the edges of the room throbbed. All the alcohol in my blood was keeping the aches and pains at bay, but I knew a world of hurt awaited me tomorrow. I wondered what was happening back at the plantation, and how long Anthony's new marriage would survive Frankie's depth charge. Maybe we deserved some guys firing a few bullets at us afterwards.

"Answer the question," I said, sharper than I intended.

"I don't know," she said. "And here's the little maudlin part: there's always the possibility I'm not here to do anything else. That I'm here for a good time, not a long time. That I'm going down like an outlaw. I'm okay with that."

"I'm not," I said, and stepping forward, I wrapped her in a clumsy embrace, crushing her close. Her hair smelled like swamp. She slapped her hands against my ribs for a few seconds before slipping her arms around me and squeezing hard. We stood like that for what felt like an eternity as the city around us boomed and screamed with life, and I already knew I'd look back at this moment and wonder if it was the last chance we'd have to make different choices, ones that wouldn't end in so much death and destruction.

PART II:
THE SHOOTING
CONTEST

1.

Back in the present, I was tapping a nonsense beat on the steering wheel while my brain revisited a sweaty, dangerous night in New Orleans. I simply couldn't think of anything to say that would encapsulate all the thoughts rushing through my head. Time grinds us all down in the end, doesn't it?

"New Orleans was 17 years ago. Anthony and his wife, they had a kid two years later," Frankie said. "That kid there. She's fifteen and you can see Anthony in her face."

The teenager had retreated up the walk to the front door of the house, which opened as she approached, revealing a stocky man in a blue suit, his muscles straining against the tailored jacket. He puffed a cigarette, its cherry casting a reddish glow into the deep valleys of his face. I recognized the gray sideburns and steely gaze.

"Percy," I said.

Frankie's widened eyes told me she'd known about the girl but not about Percy's resurrection. "It's someone else," she said. "Percy's deader than Dillinger."

"Evidently not."

Percy's eyes flicked in our direction. I sank in my seat as if that would somehow prevent him from seeing two people parked in a car less than a hundred yards away. Part of me regretted not bringing a gun. At this distance, the guy looked like he hadn't aged a day since we'd seen him die right before a massive gunfight. What the hell was going on?

"Sunlight's right on our windshield. He can't see crap," Frankie said, but wonder of wonders, her voice quavered a little.

Percy retreated into the house and shut the door.

"Maybe he has an identical twin," I said. "Like some soap opera shit."

Frankie snorted. "No."

"How do you know?"

"Because after we got back from New Orleans, I did some digging. He had a sister somewhere, no brothers. The rest of his story checked out, too, although to be fair, there wasn't much of a record, which also says something." She sighed. "I remember you didn't even bring it up again."

"Bring what up?"

"New Orleans, the wedding, any of it. We almost got shot to death on a highway and you chose to engage in your strong, silent bullshit."

"I was freaked out about it." I jabbed a finger at the windshield. "You want to give me the download on what's going on here?"

"'Give me the download.' Uh, 2004 called, it wants its lingo back." She snorted again, louder, like she was reverting to being a high schooler, using her disdain as a shield against whatever was eating her.

"Just do it," I said.

"The girl's name is Lenora. She's a huge fan of history class, anime, and video games. Nerd shit. I guess that means she's smart." She took a deep breath, held it, and exhaled. It seemed to calm her a little. "You know Anthony's dead, right?"

I startled. "What?"

"Car accident three years ago. Wife, too. They'd moved back here. No alcohol involved, according to the report I read. Just a stupid crash out on 84."

I was back at the wedding in Louisiana, watching with amusement and horror as Frankie shredded Anthony's marital bliss, Anthony's agonized face slick with sweat that looked bloody under the dance lights, his hands clenched tight into fists like he wanted to hit us. Memory is a traitor, I tried telling myself. It wasn't that bad. Anthony probably laughed it off afterwards.

Except I wondered if Anthony had ever fully recovered. I knew as well as anyone else that trauma had a way of spreading secret cracks through your soul, ready to split open at any given moment. Maybe Anthony had been driving down 84 with the lovely bride who'd never fully forgiven him for inviting those two lunatics from his hometown, and suddenly he flashed back to the wedding, his greatest humiliation, and felt there was nothing left to do but steer right into the guardrail . . .

I shook my head.

Frankie was studying my face. "Yeah," she said. "This is all really messing with you, too, huh? It took me a little time to get my head around it."

"And what's the deal here? Just tell me."

"Lenora there, she was knocked up by a very prominent local politician. This guy, he's all about the Bible and family values and whatnot, and even in these divided times, impregnating a minor would probably cost him some support."

"And put his ass in jail, hopefully."

"In this state? With his money and power? Probation at worst."

"Which politician?"

"I'll get to that," she said. "This is going to sound creepy, but I'd been keeping tabs on Anthony for years. Call it guilt if you want. I was monstrously drunk at that wedding, as you no doubt remember, but that's no excuse. When he died, I tried figuring out if I could send the daughter money, help her out in some way. Except it was like she fell off the proverbial map completely—no official guardian, no contact info, nothing. Well, I wasn't going to let that stop me. it didn't take too much digging past that to figure out what's what."

It was barely seventy degrees in the truck and yet I felt sweat trickling down the back of my neck, soaking my collar. "Have you talked to her?" I asked.

"Not yet. I wanted to scope out the security around her, get a fresh read on things."

"And you didn't know about Percy."

"Hell no. He's looking pretty good for a dead guy. When I was digging through his record way back in the day, want to hear something cool I found?"

"I assume 'cool' meant he killed some people in a spectacular way."

"Oh yeah. So, there's this guy named John Wayne Delvin, major serial killer, took out eight people in ways better not described to the faint of heart. Percy was still a cop in New Orleans, he's there when they cornered Delvin in a house. Percy decides he's gonna settle the situation by tossing a flash-bang in there. Except the house is loaded with propane tanks and explosives, and that little flash-bang sets off a chain reaction. Delvin becomes the first serial killer in orbit. It was all over the news."

"I was probably overseas when it happened. I don't remember that at all."

"In any case, Percy's always been a guy to take matters into his own hands. I have no idea how he survived, but he's here."

"Maybe he felt a debt to Anthony," I offered.

"That'd be heartwarming," she said. "Except I don't think that's the truth. I wonder if he's being paid by the governor as private security. It's the one explanation that makes sense."

"It's the governor's kid?"

She nodded. "Indeed."

"So, the governor is the daddy? You're serious?"

Governor Buddy Hunt was a lifelong politician who grew up in Caldwell, roughly a half-hour from Boise. Whenever I caught him on the local news—and he was easy to spot, because he loved wearing a ridiculous white cowboy hat too big for his head—he was shouting about imposing the death penalty for drug offenses or shooting undocumented immigrants at the state line. Over the years, I'd heard rumors that he'd played bit parts in a few softcore porn films during his college years before veering into politics.

"That's right, Mister Bible Thumper himself." She slapped my shoulder. "Don't tell me that part surprises you."

"How does this keep happening to us?" I was referring to our nasty habit of getting involved in the dirtier affairs of Idaho's richest bastards. We'd managed to kill a few over the years, but not before they used their money and influence to make our lives hell. I didn't have much interest in going toe-to-toe against the governor, who probably had a significant quantity of other rich, powerful bastards on speed dial. You can only do so much against someone who can afford an infinite number of heavily armed psychopaths.

"Because we must have pissed God off," Frankie said. "Start the car. My original plan was just to grab her after the shooting contest, give her lots of money, set her up for a new life, but Percy means there's something else going on here, and I'm not sure what the nature of it is. It creeps me out."

"Still want that Fanci Freez?"

"Nothing else will substitute."

I pulled onto Hill Road. The radio station was still on its Metallica kick, the first notes of "Enter Sandman" shaking the dashboard, and I couldn't help but think that song was totally appropriate, because Percy was a Sandman if there ever was one, yet another ruthless killer lurking in the shadows.

A milkshake with a ton of comforting sugar and fat was exactly what I needed to feel a little better. Maybe we could pull this off, I told myself. Maybe we could save this girl with no casualties or criminal charges. Maybe if we signed on for a righteous mission, the universe would reward us with good luck like a fucking karma slot machine—

Red and blue lights flashed in my rearview mirror. Rubber screeched as a black sedan swung onto the road behind us, its trunk fishtailing before its tires gripped the asphalt. As it came within kissing distance of our rear bumper, I spotted two men in the front seats, clean-cut types in suits and ties. They didn't strike me as local cops.

So much for good karma.

"Oh shit," Frankie said. "I recognize them. They're FBI."

"What should I do?" I said, already knowing the only right answer: we would need to pull over. The other alternatives were jail or a shootout. And while Frankie might have dreamed of a John Dillinger death, I had a wife and child at home. I slowed and flicked on my turn signal.

"Oh yeah," Frankie said. "I forgot to tell you, there was another reason I had to leave Mexico in a hurry."

2.

After I pulled over to the side of the road, I rolled down my window, took my driver's license from my wallet and squeezed it between my left thumb and forefinger, and placed my hands on the wheel. I didn't want a jumpy FBI agent to shoot me in the face because they thought I was reaching for a weapon.

A car door slammed behind us. "I have a gun in the glove compartment," I announced, making sure I was loud enough for anyone approaching to hear.

The agent who appeared at my window was a blonde hulk who looked like he'd played football in college and still deadlifted cars a few times per week. He wore a well-tailored gray suit that looked expensive for a government salary, along with a set of designer shades and a silk tie. He smiled and said, "Thank you for letting me know. You're Jake Halligan."

"Correct," I said, trying to find the second agent in my peripheral vision. He hovered beside Frankie's window, his left hand resting lightly on the holster strapped to his waist. He was smaller than his partner, draped in off-the-rack suit too big for his shoulders, complimented with a cheap haircut.

The blonde agent tilted his head. "Hey Frankie."

"Hey Agent Croal," Frankie said. "I wish I could say it was good to see you again, but that'd be a lie."

"Jake, my partner there is Agent Simmons," Croal said. "We're obviously acquainted with your sister. We have a proposition to discuss with you."

"Unless you have a warrant," I said, "you can shove right off."

Agent Simmons snorted.

Croal's smile twitched. "We could do it the hard way, too, but nobody wants that. Just listen to what we have to say, huh? It's a sweet deal, I promise."

It was an odd thing to hear someone in law enforcement begging for attention. Cops generally like to speak in declaratives: do this, tell us that, surrender. I glanced at Frankie, who had her left eyebrow cocked: a sign she was willing to humor these chuckleheads.

"Fine," I said. "We were on our way for milkshakes. You want us to hear what you have to say, you're buying, understand?"

Agents Croal and Simmons locked eyes for a silent conversation. After a few moments, Croal nodded and said, "Lead the way. Drive the speed limit."

I offered him the fakest of salutes before they returned to their vehicle. As I restarted the engine and angled us back onto the road, Frankie said, "I ran into Croal in Mexico. He wanted me to assassinate the head of a local cartel."

"Which you declined because you're not suicidal," I said, taking a left onto the next boulevard with its rows of stately houses and tightly cut lawns. The agents stayed a few car lengths behind us, Croal at the wheel. In the rearview I could see them talking to one another, no doubt working through whatever they would tell us.

"Exactly," she said. "And even if I succeeded in taking out this one boss—and believe me, I would've succeeded—the cartel would have just plunked someone new in his place, and that dude would have made sure I was hanging naked from an overpass by the end of the day. That aside, the deal they offered was sweet."

"Forgiveness of all your sins?"

"Oh yeah. Completely scrub my record."

"But you left."

"I figured if the FBI could find me, anyone could. I needed a reset."

"I wonder how these guys found us."

"I'm curious to know, too. As for what they want, I bet they're offering the same deal for something equally terrible." She smiled. "Maybe if I'd paid taxes for once in my life, they wouldn't be doing their best to crawl up my ass."

"You think anyone else from your past is going to pop up today?" I tried to make a joke out of it, but my nerves were jangled. It reminded me too much of those horrible days when we were pursued by the richest man in the state and his psychopathic friends, everything solid I'd believed about the world shaking apart around me.

"God, I hope not," Frankie said. "Fortunately, we've blown up a lot of the folks who have a grudge against us."

She had a good point.

We were fighters.

Someone might take us down, but not before we drew a lot of blood.

Still, the idea of leaving my family behind made me nauseous.

Ahead of us, a traffic light flashed yellow. I hit the gas, wondering what our new friends would do. I made it through the intersection with a millisecond to spare. Croal's siren blared as he ran the light, but he kept his distance for the rest of the trip to Fanci Freez. The Freez was an old-school diner on the corner of W State and N 14th that had served Boise's best burgers and shakes for as long as I could remember. It was crowded as usual, the drive-through clogged with cars, a line of kids at the outside order window.

I pulled into the parking lot and found an empty space near the drive-through entrance. By the time we exited the car, Croal had parked at the curb. He and Simmons looked infuriated as they emerged, as if it took all their self-control to not cuff us to the pavement after my little stunt with the light. I found that amusing.

"Get us two peanut butter and chocolate milkshakes, large," Frankie called to them as she secured one of the large outdoor tables.

Simmons reddened but they kept walking. They returned from the order window with two milkshakes and two small sodas in a cardboard tray. "Thank you," I said as Croal passed our drinks to us.

"You're welcome," Croal said in his most deadpan voice. "Are we done with the crap? Can we talk?"

But Simmons wasn't ready to give it up. "You're just a pair of rednecks who're good at shooting people," he snapped, as if he'd been saving that one up since the traffic stop.

"I take umbrage at that statement," I told him.

Croal smirked. "That's a good word. Where did you go to school?"

"Just the school of hard knocks," I said. "But I'm a big reader."

Simmons stared at the ground while sucking on his straw.

"Cute, very cute." Croal grinned to show how cute it was. "I went to school in Cambridge."

"He's referring to Harvard," Frankie said. "For some reason, none of them can actually say the word 'Harvard.' They have to act like they're being discreet about it, say 'in Cambridge,' but believe me, he really wants you to know."

Croal's grin fell like a defective rocket. "Yes, Harvard. And you know what I learned there?"

It was Frankie's turn to smile. "How to bugger other people in your dorm?" she asked sweetly.

"You better watch your mouth," Simmons growled.

Croal raised a hand. "No, it's okay. That was pretty funny." His eyes said he didn't find it funny at all. "We learned that it doesn't matter who's right or moral or whatever, just as long as they're the one with the money."

"Somehow I don't think you got that from Kant," I said.

"People keep telling us they know all about money and power," Frankie said. "But if we're talking about what we've learned, you know what I've learned? All the money and power in the world can't stand up to a ten-cent bullet."

"Which is exactly why we're here," Croal said. "Thanks for the seamless transition. The pregnant girl? We've had her under surveillance for weeks. We were sitting up on that hill, you know, with a view of the road and the house. Imagine our surprise when we see you two pull up. My luck's been good lately, and—"

"You weren't nearly this verbose in Mexico," Frankie said.

Croal sighed. "We know the governor's responsible for knocking her up. We'd like you to—"

"We're not going to shoot her," I said.

Croal shook his head. "Not what we want. Quite the opposite, in fact. What's your connection to her?"

"All you need to know," Frankie said, "is we intend to get her out of that situation."

"Excellent," Croal said. "And what better way to do that than getting her to reveal the whole thing on a prominent news site? We have a sympathetic journalist ready to hear her story. We just need someone to deliver her to the meet."

"Why not do it yourselves?" I asked. "You're the FBI. You can march right in there."

"I bet this isn't on the books," Frankie mock-whispered to me. "Just like the cartel thing."

"She's right," Croal told me. "The governor's debating whether to run for the highest office in the land. Let's just say that a few good folks in positions of power see him as a real threat, and they'd appreciate if he were . . . neutered. I don't think he'd make it through the primaries, personally—the guy is a clown—but clowns sometimes do more than you expect."

"And if we do this, my record's scrubbed?" Frankie asked. "Same deal as before?"

"You blew up someone with a rocket launcher," Simmons said, almost to himself.

Frankie raised a finger. "*Allegedly helped* blow up someone with a rocket launcher. I pulled no such trigger. Let's be careful with our wording."

"And if we don't agree," I said, "you retaliate, right?"

"You think you could kill who you've killed and just walk? That kind of money never forgets." Croal shrugged like he was offering the world's most obvious truth. "Who's to say there's not an ongoing investigation?"

"Is there?" I asked, feeling like someone had punched me lightly in the stomach.

He shrugged, more theatrically this time. "If there is, and it goes nuclear, the legal bills will eat you alive. Plus, who's to say you wouldn't end up facing a lot of felony charges? But that won't be my problem, will it?"

Frankie's hands had disappeared beneath the table. I remembered the Beretta in her belly holster. The FBI guys hadn't bothered to frisk us. They probably thought they were fast on the draw, but Frankie could clear her pistol and put two in each of their heads in a quarter-second.

The FBI guys sensed it. Simmons lowered his drink and let his hands rest on his thighs. He tried to be casual about it. Croal smiled and spread his hands, and I heard a faint scrape of a sole on concrete as he adjusted his stance. If Frankie tried something, I bet he would try to kick her, because that's what I would do if I couldn't draw my firearm fast enough.

Frankie flicked her gaze to me. I tilted my head toward the little kids clustered around the restaurant's outdoor order window. Her hands reappeared atop the table. I nodded slightly.

"One other thing," Frankie said. "You have any idea who's guarding the girl? A little info on that front could come in helpful. Since you've been watching her for so long and all."

Croal paused. "You just need to know they're armed and willing to use force. Are you in or out?"

"You got a number I can call you?" Frankie said. "We need to think about it."

Croal nodded and drew a business card from his pocket as he stood. "Sure," he said, tossing the card on the table. "Don't think too long, got it?"

"Yeah," Simmons added, his voice rising like an angry kid on the playground. "Got it?"

"Oh yeah, we got it," Frankie said, the fingers on her right hand flexing like a gunfighter warming up.

3.

On the way back to the house, Frankie drummed her fingers on her knees, her eyes flicking over the traffic snarling the highway out of Boise.

"I love how everything in our lives is always so simple," I said, sipping my milkshake. "So easy and straightforward."

She struggled not to grin. "Oh yeah. Nobody has it easier than us."

"You think those FBI guys were serious about an investigation? Or were they just fucking with us?"

The grin died in mid-takeoff. "Do I think there's an investigation? Absolutely. Rich people don't die without the cops poking at the reasons why, even if it's been years. Do I think we're named in that investigation? Maybe. But if things get too public, it might raise too many questions that folks don't want answered, you know? Especially political folks."

"If it gets too public, someone might try to kill us," I said. "Again, that is."

I was thinking about my father, how he had tried to stand for justice in its purest and uncut form, never taking a bribe or looking the other way, and it had cost him everything in the end. How he told me once he'd do it all over again, because what was a man without their principles? Not for the first time, I wondered if Frankie had grown up a criminal and gun runner as a reaction to his righteousness, the way that kids of liberal parents sometimes turned ragingly conservative. Or maybe that was too simple—maybe my sister had been born with a dark soul.

But what about me? I'd tried so long to live by my father's example, and the world had laughed in my face and said: *Who cares?* I felt like I'd earned a lifetime of trouble simply by breathing.

"—bro," Frankie said.

I shook my head, snapping back to reality. "Sorry, what?" I asked.

"I said: This time, they might actually be smart about it, arrest us, then Epstein us, bro." She mimed being strangled. "Which means we need to do something."

"What?"

An 18-wheeler rumbled past in the right lane, a steel wall that blocked out the sun, casting us into deep shadow. "I really have to win that shooting match," she said. "If we have money, we have leverage, opportunity. And if we don't have that, we're dead."

4.

The night before the shooting match, when Frankie disappeared into the fields to center herself and talk to whatever demons lived in her head, I opened my gun locker and cleaned the pistols and double-checked that I had plenty of ammunition and spare cash. I even opened the medical kit on the locker's bottom shelf and made sure it was still loaded with Israeli tourniquets and gauze pads soaked in blood-clotting agent.

When I closed the locker, I placed my forehead against its cool metal and commanded myself to breathe in, hold it for four seconds, breathe out. I was already too nervous. How had I ever survived Iraq? Or the violence I'd seen back home? Maybe I'd been a different person back then. Maybe I was much weaker these days.

I retreated to the kitchen, where I made myself a protein smoothie in the little blender. I tried to push back on the darkness in my mind by telling myself it would all work out. Frankie was one of the best shooters I'd ever seen in my life, if not the best, and she would nail all her targets and win the big prize. I would use the winnings to pay off our loans and Ivan. And after that, we would figure out about Anthony's kid and why she was guarded by a man who should have died on a lonely highway years ago—

The darker thoughts grew stronger. Too many things needed to go right. The difference between success and death was Frankie shooting a target roughly an inch across, and at however many yards, with the wind picking up, anything could happen—

"Shut up and drink your smoothie," I muttered.

"What?" Janine called from the stairs.

"Nothing," I said. "Just being crazy."

She stepped into view, leaning against the kitchen doorway with her arms crossed over her chest. "What's bothering you?"

I still hadn't told her anything about Ivan or Anthony's kid or how I was betting our future on Frankie's marksmanship, and I realized that was part of what was driving me insane. How much had we been through together? I'd trust her with my life, so why not this?

"Nothing," I said, hating myself as the word drifted through the air.

She frowned. "You're sure?"

"Yeah. I'm just nervous for Frankie. There's that shooting competition tomorrow."

"She seems nervous about it, too." She cocked her head. "Are you betting on it?"

"Yeah, but just a couple bucks." It's easier to tell a half-truth than a total lie.

"Then I hope you win, even if it's just a bit of cash." Her gaze shifted to the floor. "I think we should put it toward the credit cards because the interest—"

"I know, I know," I snapped. "You don't need to keep bring up the bills over and over—"

"I'm not—"

"Yes. Yes, you're spiraling." Except I was the one spiraling, my dark thoughts building like a thunderhead. I was back on that highway in Louisiana, ankle-deep in mud while shadows swarmed at the edges of my vision, readying to tear me apart. "We're doing the best we can, okay?"

"I'm not saying we're not." She raised her hands. "I was just saying, okay? I didn't mean anything by it. I'm sorry."

Her miserable frown short-circuited my anger, and suddenly I felt a deep shame, the kind that makes you want to walk outside and set yourself on fire. This was the mother of my child, the person I'd chosen to spend my life with. "I'm sorry, too," I said.

She stepped close, her head on my chest, and I wrapped my arms around her. She was warm and her heartbeat tap-tap-tapped against my sternum. I kissed the top of her head, loving the honeysuckle smell of her shampoo. "I can't believe you're drinking that protein stuff," she murmured into my shirt. "It makes you fart like a wildebeest."

"It helps keep me going," I said. "I'll do my best not to toot around you."

"No, it's okay. I had that leftover barbeque for lunch, so I plan on giving as good as I get."

I laughed and kissed her again. "If that's the way it's got to be."

I was proud of how I kept my expression neutral because I felt worse, almost sadistic. I loved her and kept lying to her, and if those lies came to light, it would only wound her more deeply.

5.

We pulled onto Crazy Bill's ranch an hour before the match commenced and found the gravel lot off the driveway already filled with trucks and SUVs. I spotted a few Punisher and black-and-white flag decals on rear windows, along with bumper stickers with trenchant bits of advice like, "ANNOY A LIBERAL = BE HAPPY" and '1/144,000.' I rumbled into a slot at the lot's furthest edge, beside the barbed-wire fence and ditch that separated the ranch from the main road.

"We missed our opportunity," Frankie said. "We could have slapped an 'I LOVE MARX' bumper sticker on your truck, gave someone a heart attack."

"I don't like putting anything on my truck," I said.

"Yeah, because you're no fun."

"No, because I don't like anything too identifiable." I shut off the engine and leaned back, enjoying the air conditioning for another moment. My rearview mirror framed black duffel bag on the back seat, its sides bulging with cash. My nerves crackled.

Frankie was dressed for success in a black t-shirt with the sleeves cut off, along with lightweight black pants and a leather hip holster. When she used to compete in shooting contests on the regular, she would always wear one of our dad's old baseball caps, and I had managed to scrounge up his gray one with a frayed strap from a box in my bedroom closet.

I hoped it would bring her luck.

We needed it.

She must have sensed my tension because she took my hand and squeezed it. "I'm going to win," she said. "I promise. I don't fail."

"I know you don't," I said, squeezing back.

We exited into the heat of the day. Frankie retrieved her gun case from the back seat while I fetched the duffel bag, sweeping my gaze over the chaos beyond the lot. There were enough armed men on these acres to launch an invasion of Cuba. The .45 strapped to my hip was puny compared to their AR-15s and other high-caliber rifles.

Crazy Bill's property was anchored on its western edge by his redneck mansion, an enormous pile of weather-beaten wood with a wraparound porch and a fenced-in yard prickly with cheatgrass and broken bottles. For a rich man, he sure wasn't interested in fresh paint or landscaping. A hundred yards of hard-packed dirt, dotted with rusted cars and other wreckage, separated his crumbling residence from the range.

"What a waste," Frankie said. "Give me property like this, I'm installing a hot tub, some solar panels at the very least."

"Slobs gonna slob," I said, wondering what Frankie truly thought about the chaos of my homestead.

Beside the range stood a shipping container with a rectangular hole cut in its flank. Two teenage girls in tank tops stood inside, pouring plastic cups of beer from a line of kegs, then handing the cups to the thirty-odd people clustered outside. The air pulsed with the heavy bass of stadium country from two enormous speakers set on the container's roof, not the good shit like Johnny Cash but generic rah-rah crap written by a frat boy who probably lived in a fancy house in New York between concert tours.

I studied the range. From a beaten-down shed, contestants stepped onto a narrow yard of white sand lined by oil-smeared traffic cones. They were expected to sweep from right to left, nailing shredded mannequins and tin targets while doing their best to avoid the blue barrels and rusted-out cars.

Someone on Crazy Bill's staff had placed a wire cage with five propane tanks along the side of the shed, beside a pair of rusted-out oxygen canisters and a barrel smeared with something black that could have been oil. You'd only need one ricochet from the course—or heck, some idiot tripping hard and firing accidentally as they fell—to transform the shed into a massive bomb. So much for safety.

Next, I scanned the crowd. Most of the folks in that crowd looked like me: thick, tattooed, bearded, dressed in camo and black. I bet the majority had served in one of the sandboxes on the other side of the world. But my eye was drawn to the four men standing at the range entrance. Three of them were thin guys rigged up with camera and sound recording gear, while the fourth was bulked up with gym muscles and clad in ultra-expensive tactical gear, his eyes hidden behind mirrored shades. He ranted and raved into the cameras for a few moments, paused, adjusted his stance, and did it again. I couldn't quite hear his speechifying at this distance.

"That's Eric Sears," Frankie said. "He's a big deal on YouTube."

"What's he do on YouTube?"

"You haven't heard of him? I'm shocked."

"I don't think I've turned on my laptop in a year."

"He reviews firearms. Like, long reviews, twenty minutes of him blathering about everything down to the firing pins. They eat it up online—millions of views. He also posts video of him on the range. He acts like he's former Special Forces."

"Was he military?" I squinted against the fierce sunlight. Eric Sears was jabbing a finger at one of his cameramen and screaming, his voice almost a squeal over the wind whistling across the range. I caught something about sponsorships and heads in asses.

She snorted. "I think he played paintball a bunch of times, that's how close he's actually come to combat."

"Here's the key question: Is he a good shot?"

She shrugged. "Everybody here's a good shot. But he won't win."

I served as Frankie's caddie, carrying the gun case up the dusty trail to the range, the money bag looped over my shoulder. As we approached, Crazy Bill emerged from his house, arms spread wide, howling in lunatic joy as he wove past the barrels and rusted-out engine parts scattered across his property. He looked like an aging biker, his gray beard dangling at his belt, his thick body clad in scuffed leather and torn denim. Maybe he thought that outfit made him just one of the guys, but his money crackled around him like electricity, changing how everyone looked at him.

Crazy Bill spied Frankie and his eyes widened. "Oh shit!" he yelled. "This competition just got interesting! The one and only Frankie, back from the dead!"

The crowd shifted its focus to my sister, who grinned and waggled her fingers like a sorority girl entering a party. But most of them knew who she was, and she knew they knew it. Some of the closer men hardened their stares, which only made her bubblier: she hopped from foot to foot, waving her hands above her head, as if a cheerleading squad was shouting her name with glee.

I tensed, because men don't like being mocked, and even Frankie's fearsome reputation might not prevent one of these shooters from doing something dumb. Did any law-enforcement agency have a reward for her capture? Or, God help us, did a cartel have a bounty on her head? A single phone call could transform this into a very bad day.

If Crazy Bill had hired security, they were indistinguishable from the contestants, maybe by design. I clocked a pair of clean-cut guys in crisp fatigues leaning against the container, pegging them as Army, maybe even JSOC. The guys were grinning, which was a good sign—too many people at these events took things too seriously.

"Place your bets," Frankie called to the assembled. "If I win, first round of drinks is on me."

That was smart of her: take the edge off the crowd. I was reminded of our meeting with the FBI guys, and how Frankie had sat there with her milkshake and knocked Agent Croal off-balance by making jokes about Harvard sodomy. She was good at reading people. That's why she'd survived so long as a gunrunner, not a profession known for its longevity.

Eric Sears, the YouTuber, wandered over, trailed by his camera crew. "Who're you?" he asked Frankie.

"I'm nobody," she said. "Who're you?" It was her favorite response to that question, stolen from Emily Dickinson. She'd used it for years, and we had yet to encounter anyone at a gun show or bar who knew it—except for Boz, her ex, but he was long dead.

"I'm the guy who's going to win this contest." Eric pivoted toward his cameras, his voice rising an octave, sounding now like an announcer who'd chugged too many energy drinks. "And can you believe it, you're going to watch me do it with an absolutely badass rifle that I just cannot wait to break down for you later, it's going to be awesome, folks, it's going to blow your mind like nobody's business!"

With that, he unslung the weapon from behind his back. It looked like something a Martian stormtrooper might wield in a Paul Verhoeven sci-fi film, a bright gold AR-15 studded out with a drum magazine, massive scope, laser sight, and—I couldn't believe what I was seeing—a small pair of brass nuts dangling from the grip.

"Yeah, that's not compensating for anything," Frankie said, and before Eric could say anything, she tilted her head to the cameras. "Are you live? Streaming to all your fans?"

"You bet we are. We got a countdown going and everything." Eric smirked. "The countdown to when I kick your sweet little ass. Want to make a side bet on it?"

"This is amazing!" Frankie said, breaking into a broad smile for however many thousands of gun enthusiasts were staring at their phones and laptops at this very moment. "I always wanted to appear on the YouTube channel devoted to the world's smallest dick!"

Eric's head snapped back as if punched. He clearly wasn't used to anyone talking to him like that. "Excuse me?"

I quietly set down the gun case. I hooked my thumbs into my waistband, my right hand close to my holstered pistol. Frankie had slipped into chaos mode, which meant the chances of me needing to put a bullet in someone's knee were rising steadily. *Come on*, I wanted to tell her. *We have money we need to win.*

Except if I said anything, it might knock Frankie off her game, make her seem weak, and these guys would smell it. I didn't want to think about anyone watching the livestream who could identify her. How many people from her old life knew she was back from Mexico?

Frankie leaned closer to the lenses, going for her extreme closeup as her voice dipped to a conspiratorial whisper. "I heard if Eric Sears ran into a wall with a boner, he'd break his nose."

Eric's crew circled her, and I spotted one of them trying not to laugh. I bet they didn't like him very much. Eric's hands flexed on his rifle's stock, the little balls swinging in the breeze. I was ready if he tried something stupid.

"You can joke all you want," Eric said quietly, leaning close enough to kiss her. "But I'm going to make you beg out there. On your knees—"

He grunted, his back snapping ramrod-straight, because Frankie had a hand between his legs and was squeezing as hard as she could, the tendons in her forearms straining like overtaxed bridge cables. "How about you get on yours?" she asked cheerfully.

I glimpsed the phone screen held by one of the circling camera crew: the feed had a hundred thousand viewers and rising rapidly, the lower-right corner a blur of numbers and thumbs-up emojis.

"Hey there," offered a relaxed voice behind me.

I shifted slightly to see the speaker. It was one of the JSOC-looking guys with a tight red beard. He was smiling, a plastic cup of beer in his left hand, but nothing about the smile was friendly. I sensed the guy was ready for violence, but only if someone else kicked it off. That was the kind of head-crunching I could get behind, so I gave him a little nod.

He returned the gesture.

Good. He might help if this went weird.

"Hey," Frankie said to the JSOC guy without looking behind her. She twisted her hand along with Eric's balls. Eric squealed like a pig on helium.

"My name is Barrett," the JSOC guy said, as if we were hanging out in a bar and Frankie wasn't turning a guy's gonads to a fine paste. "And I appreciate that you're having a disagreement here. But let's save our aggression for the range, okay?"

"This guy annoys me," Frankie offered.

"Hey, I hate his YouTube channel, too." Barrett shrugged. "He's a huge poser. But leave his ass-kicking for out there, okay? All this animosity is making everyone nervous, and that's not what we want."

"Good word," I said.

He shifted his attention to me. "Which one?"

"Animosity."

Crazy Bill edged into my field of view; his soft hands raised to the sky. "Everybody, when Crazy Bill tells you things are getting a little too crazy, maybe you better listen, hey?" he warbled. "Hey?"

"Girl, how about we make a deal here?" Barrett said. "You let go of that wimpy YouTuber's nuts, I buy you a drink—they got whiskey back there, too, not just beer—and he promises not to do anything stupid. That sound good to everyone?"

"Sure," Frankie said, releasing her grip.

Eric stumbled back, bowlegged, hissing between clenched teeth. His hands scrabbled at his crotch, as if checking that everything was intact, before darting to his rifle. His pain was draining away, replaced by pink-cheeked rage.

I gripped my pistol, ready to draw.

Eric's gaze flicked to me.

I knew he saw the murder in my eyes.

His finger tapped his rifle's trigger guard.

He tried to smile—it was more of a pained grimace—and spun to face his camera crew, which had continued broadcasting his humiliation to every gun nut and video-game nerd on Earth. They knew he'd fire them all by the end of the day, and their grins said they were totally cool with that outcome.

"Like I was saying," he told the cameras, trying to switch to his ultra-chipper host voice, but the best he could do was a raspy squeak, "we going to give you a hell of a show out on the range! I love this competition here! Love, love, love it!"

Frankie winked at Eric as he slithered away, the camera crew trailing a few feet behind. Once he reached the parking lot, she leaned against the side of the shipping container and exhaled. "I'll take a water," she told Barrett. "I'm not dumb enough to drink before an event this big."

Barrett smiled. "It was worth a shot, so to speak. I figured I'd squeeze any advantage I could get."

The crowd had returned to their conversations and equipment checks, some of them sparing us a glance every few seconds. A few had lined up to pass wads of cash to the girls behind the bar. The handwritten sign above the beer keg read, 'Place Yer Bets Here.'

I had to place my bet, too. The duffel bag felt like it weighed two hundred pounds as I lined up with the other miscreants. This is your last chance, I thought. You could walk away, find another solution, not bet your family on Frankie nailing a little paper target.

As I made my way toward the front of the line, I had a new angle on the bar's interior and the whiteboard on the back wall, with its grid of bettors and how much they'd put down. Some folks had placed two hundred grand on their champion to win, which meant they could walk away with more than I'd earned in a decade of bounty hunting.

How would I feel if I had a chance at that kind of fortune—and squandered it because of cowardice?

Frankie was the best shooter here, wasn't she?

I arrived at the bar counter, bag's thick canvas strap slick in my sweaty hands. *Last chance to back out*, squealed the cowardly part of my brain. *Last chance, last chance, last chance . . .*

An enormous gong boomed behind me, startling that voice away. Crazy Bill tilted his enormous head to the endless blue sky and hollered, spittle flying from his lips in ropes: *"Folks, five minutes! Then we commence to shooting!"*

Behind the bar, a thin girl with dry brown hair offered a wary smile as I heaved the bag onto the counter. "I'm feeling good today," I told her, but there was a tightness to my voice, as if I was crouched in a bunker, artillery screaming above, death breathing against the back of my neck.

6.

I took a position among the crowd to the left of the range, where I had a sweeping view of the targets and cover. Crazy Bill had designed the course so each contestant would need to move rapidly to the left once the buzzer sounded, trying to sight the targets squeezed between barrels and tucked behind vertical pieces of rebar rammed into the hard soil. If not for Crazy Bill's little tricks, it wouldn't be that difficult a course for someone who knew what they were doing.

And the contestants knew what they were doing. Barrett was first in the lineup. He shot like a JSOC guy, methodical in his movements, pausing a microsecond after each shot to verify whether he'd hit. It made him a bit slower than the competition shooters who'd never been in combat, but he nailed everything he saw, and in close contests like this one, that could easily be enough. Slow is smooth and smooth is fast.

Barrett left the course grinning.

"He's pretty good," I told Frankie beside me. "You should ask him for a date."

"I've known enough meatheads in my day," she said. "But his ass is intriguing."

"Maybe you can take him out when you win. Spring for a fancy meal."

"I'll let him order an extra patty on his burger."

I laughed. "Big spender."

Three husky men in bullet-resistant vests and camo approached the side of the shipping container. The girls behind the bar heaved five massive duffel bags onto the counter, which creaked and popped beneath the weight. Two of the men shouldered the bags while the third faced the crowd, his hand on the pistol holstered to his waist. This was Crazy Bill's security.

The men with the bags grunted their way toward Crazy Bill's house, the third spreading out so he could watch them and the crowd at the same time. Everyone else focused on the shooter after Barrett, a weekend warrior in brand-new gear who messed up on his first targets and spent the rest of his time laughing in anger while blasting at random parts of the landscape.

Frankie offered the departing security a significant look, then waggled her eyebrows at me. "Lot of cash in play. It's a miracle nobody's tried to knock this contest off."

"Simple," I said. "Too many guys with guns. Not just Crazy Bill's guys, but also everyone who doesn't want their money disappearing. You wouldn't make it out of the parking lot."

"Correction, most guys wouldn't make it out of the parking lot." She jabbed a thumb at her chest. "I would make it out. Why am I even participating in the contest? We should just take the money and run. How secure could that house really be?"

A few feet away, a bearded giant turned to study us. I stared him off. "I don't think they appreciate our sense of humor,"

I said. "Besides, you have enough people gunning for you already."

"True." She nodded at the course. "Check out this dude."

The next guy was six feet of beer belly and stubble and bad attitude. Like many of the other shooters, he had an expensive kit so new it practically had the sales tags still hanging from it, but unlike those amateurs who thought they had a shot at the title, he drew down at the buzzer with impressive speed. If he'd lived during the Wild West, he might have rocked the frontier towns as a famous duelist. Whatever his chances of winning now, they lasted the three seconds until Crazy Bill triggered a big trick.

The contestant was aiming at the first targets, a trio of bullet-riddled mannequin torsos, when a theatrical geyser of dirt exploded to his left. From the gritty cloud popped a clown with a bright red wig and a pair of yellow overalls, his gloved hands clutching what looked like a pink Uzi. The clown unleashed a piercing shriek that sounded like a dozen crows stuck in a piece of industrial machinery.

The shooter hesitated, and I could almost read his thoughts: was that a person dressed up as a clown, or an animatronic dummy? Should I—

The clown's dirt-streaked arms jerked to life and its Uzi erupted in noisy flame. The crowd ducked and a few people screamed.

Frankie laughed and shook her head. "You amateurs," she shouted. "Those are blanks."

The shooter had lowered his pistol slightly. Now he raised it again—his hands shaking—and emptied the rest of his clip into the clown's head, which exploded in plastic shards. A black, boxy speaker tumbled from the wreckage and thumped in the dirt, still emitting that ungodly shriek.

From somewhere behind me, Crazy Bill cackled.

The shooter fired another four times to destroy the speaker, then completed his run like a professional—except his aim was off, and he left too many of the more distant targets untouched as he left the course. I had to resist pumping my fist. Everyone who failed out there was one less person who could take this prize from Frankie.

I just hoped Crazy Bill didn't activate something insane when it was her turn.

"Two more until me. I should head in," Frankie said, clapping me on the shoulder before disappearing into the shed. I was so nervous I barely paid attention to the next two shooters who swept through the course, scoring decent but unspectacular runs.

Then Frankie appeared.

As she stood on the starting mark, hunched slightly in her ready stance, her hand drifting over her holster, I saw—or I thought I saw—a slight tremble in her thumb. Maybe it was just a trick of the light. Maybe it was Frankie's nerves, the ones she kept joking about. It was enough to send a fresh jolt of fear through my already overtaxed system, and I did my best to breathe through it in the forever seconds before her run began.

When the buzzer sounded, Frankie drew and pivoted, smooth and sleek, pumping rounds into targets, hitting every mannequin and target dead-center. She moved more like the JSOC boys than the competition shooters, pausing for a microsecond after each hit, but her transitions between shooting and moving were also looser than the military version, less drilled. With every passing second, I felt my tension ease, because she was hitting everything she needed to hit dead-center, reloading so fast her empty magazine didn't even hit the ground before the full one was slotted into her weapon, and I thought: yes, finally for once we're going to pull this off, this big gamble—

With a shuddering bang, purple smoke burst from the ground to her left, followed by a red and yellow flash rocketing skyward. She was already midway through popping five bottles set up atop a barrel, her finger tightening on the trigger, and at least one of her shots went wild because the last two bottles were still intact as she popped the magazine and reloaded, her head turning to evaluate whatever was flying through the air—another one of Crazy Bill's fucking clown dolls—and she shifted the pistol toward this new target, maybe because it was her instinct to gun down whatever was moving within her sightline, or maybe she wanted to score bonus points by knocking it out of the sky, but whatever her reasons she missed four shots as the clown skidded face-down in the dirt, and that was it, I knew we were screwed: in a competition like this, one or two missed shots was the difference between taking home all the cash or leaving empty-handed.

It was all over.

My house.

My loans.

My trigger fingers.

My *marriage*.

Frankie spent the next twenty seconds clearing the rest of the targets, bang-bang-bang, and as she finished she turned toward me. Her gaze was cold.

I knew what was coming next: bad decisions, deaths.

My money was already gone.

My marriage was next, because I would need to tell Janine everything.

We'd have to kill Ivan. Or he'd have to kill us.

And Frankie's mission to save Anthony's child? Scrubbed before it even began. Sorry, kid.

All this destruction because I thought I was smart.

More gunshots erupted—but not from the range, where Frankie was still standing, her beautiful pistol loose in her left hand.

No, they were coming from behind us.

I dropped to one knee, my pistol already out. Something very bad was happening, bigger than an argument over drinks or a side bet. We were under attack.

7.

From my crouch I scuttled for the side of the shipping container. Its thin metal sides would block any high-velocity round about as effectively as a sheet of paper, so I hoped that whoever had stocked the bar had lined the inside with lots of heavy kegs and coolers. I press-checked my pistol to verify a round in the chamber and peeked around the container's edge.

It was chaos across the range. You could instantly tell which competitors had served in the military: like me, they'd dropped and found suitable cover within a few milliseconds. I spotted our new JSOC friends crouched alongside the shed. Frankie was nowhere in sight—knowing her, she was probably inside the shed, helping herself to fresh magazines and any other toys that looked promising.

More automatic fire ripped the air—multiple shooters, all of them to my right.

A sizable portion of the crowd descended into panic. Some ran for their cars and others decided to play Rambo, pointing their weapons at anything that might be a threat. Something buzz-snapped past my face like a hypersonic bee, followed by the pop of a small-caliber pistol, and I ducked back.

"WE'RE BEIN' ROBBED!" Crazy Bill yelled from somewhere beyond the shipping container. "ROBBED!"

Frankie was right: all that money was too tempting for someone to resist.

I'd have thought twice before trying to knock off a target filled with some of the most heavily armed and competent shooters in the state, but hey, most criminals are stone-cold idiots. That's why they're criminals and not living a normal life.

Frankie burst from the doorway of the shed and sprinted toward me in a crouch, her rifle socked against her shoulder, her waistband heavy with new magazines. Dirt exploded beside her feet—either a stray shot or someone aiming at her—and she dove and rolled. I scooted backwards as she skidded next to me and spun so she faced outward, raising the rifle. "Hold on," she said, scanning for targets. "I can't see who did that. Fucking idiots."

My brain had clicked into that hyper-alert state, opening the adrenaline tap until my heart sped at a million miles an hour, my thoughts moving faster. I could smell the dust kicked up by scrambling feet, sense the bullets carving the air as more people fired wildly, hear the screams of pain as those bullets impacted. Part of me loved it. I'd never admit something like that to anyone who'd never experienced combat, but I loved it.

"It's okay," I said. "I bet we can go for a disqualification."

"Ha, you're fucking funny." She lowered her weapon slightly as she peeked around the side of the container. "Parking lot is a mess. Something's going on down there. Couldn't really see, though."

A gentleman with a waist-length beard and sunglasses was sprinting toward us, hands flailing in panic, as if he meant to crowd onto our bit of cover. I tucked aside to give him space, but Frankie raised the rifle an inch, maybe to warn him off. Not that it mattered: the right side of the man's head exploded, his knees went horribly loose, and his body flopped facedown to the dust. To his left, a woman with dry blonde hair and a fanny pack dropped her smoking .45, slapped her hands over her mouth, and screamed.

"The fuck was she shooting at?" Frankie said.

Impulse, I almost said, before a fresh burst of automatic gunfire erupted from the parking lot, punctuated by a scatter of pistol shots and a shotgun blast.

"ROBBED!" Crazy Bill roared again.

Barrett and his friend crouched behind the shed. I waved for him to come over, and he waited for his moment before sprinting across, his buddy on his heels. They thumped into the gap between me and Frankie, breathing hard. "What a shit show," Barrett said.

"You have a view from down there?" Frankie asked.

The metal above our heads sparked, followed by the whine of a ricochet singing into the sky. Another flurry of shots plowed into the shed, blasting wood into puffs of dust.

Barrett shook his head. "It's a bad angle between here and the house, but whatever's happening, it's over there. The parking lot, too."

"What's the plan?" Barrett's buddy asked.

A wisp of gray smoke drifted from the door of the shed, followed by a shimmer of superheated air.

"Stay here. At least it's cover," I said, even as I spied the tongue of flame, almost invisible against the brightness of the day, flicking from the doorway of the shed. That burst of bullets must have hit something flammable inside.

"Gasoline," Frankie said, following my gaze. "There were a couple cans in there. Oh yeah, and a lot of ammo, too."

"Plus, propane on the side there," Barrett added. "Oh shit."

Dark smoke poured from gaps in the shed's roof. The shipping container was no more than twenty yards away, and if those propane and oxygen tanks exploded, the shrapnel would shred us to pieces. "We better move," I said.

"Where?" Frankie said. "It's a bullet storm out there."

She had a point.

"Hold on," I said. Staying low, my pistol tucked against my body, I scooted to the opposite edge of the shipping container. I spotted Eric Sears and his YouTube crew behind a rusted Ford sedan in the no man's land between the shipping container and the house. I'd noticed the car as we walked in, and dismissed it as a hunk of junk, but from my new angle I could see that its tires were worn but inflated, most of its dusty windows intact. Maybe Crazy Bill used it to tool around his property instead of an ATV.

Eric was shrieking into the cameras, and while the crackle of flames and ammunition made his spiel hard to hear, I caught, "make sure to hit that button and subscribe!" before a fresh burst of heavy fire chewed up the Ford's hood.

Eric yelped and flattened to the dirt.

I had a better angle on the house. Two figures clad in body armor and WARQ helmets stood on the porch steps, cradling what looked like Heckler & Koch G36KV rifles. A moment later, three more followed, taking positions behind the porch furniture and railings. At this distance, with their shiny equipment and their heads covered, they looked like androids from a science-fiction movie. Bits of porch burst into the air as they exchanged fire with the crowd. A flash and boom, and the initial duo disappeared through the front door.

Who was crazy enough to rob a shooting contest?

With more than a million dollars in cash on the property, that list of suspects was very long. Except most of them would have tried to execute this little caper in some almost unfathomably stupid way, like charging in drunk with two pistols. Whoever these guys were, they were professional, almost certainly ex-military . . .

"Bro," Frankie yelled.

I pivoted on my heel. The shed's roof was dissolving in flame.

"On me," I said, flattened my hand and chopped in the direction of the rusted car where the YouTubers had taken shelter. Nothing else in my view would block bullets effectively. I could only hope Eric didn't do something stupid once we reached him. If he decided this was the perfect time to make Frankie pay for humiliating him earlier . . .

Then Eric did something amazing.

And by 'amazing,' I mean completely idiotic.

"Let's get this done!" Eric shouted, and, rising to a crouch, darted toward the house, firing his ultra-expensive rifle as he moved. His frightened YouTube crew remained in place, sticking their cameras over the Ford's chewed bulk, the better to capture their dear leader's last moments on the planet.

Because here's the issue with most of these gun YouTubers: they want you to believe they've endured combat, that they're gurus of gunfire who know everything possible about ending a life, but the reality is they haven't killed anything other than a deer, maybe. They've paid a lot of money to attend those weekend "boot camps" where they crawl in the mud beneath tangles of barbed wire and do a few house-clearing drills, but they've never had to face off against people who want to kill them.

Eric moved well, so well that the uninitiated might have confused him for an operator who'd done a few tours in Africa and the Middle East, but he had no idea about how to use cover to save his ass in the middle of a firefight. Marching out in the open, in the bright sunlight, was something you saw in movies. In real life, it was a quick way to turn your body into a bullet sponge.

Eric fired in controlled bursts, swiveling his barrel slightly as he found new targets, which allowed him to survive for all of twenty feet before a half-dozen shots smashed into him, knocking him off his feet, his left boot tumbling into the air.

His camera crew looked embarrassed.

But in dying, Eric had done us a solid, distracting everyone long enough for us to dive for cover behind the Ford.

"I bet that gets a billion views," Frankie said, slapping one of the camera guys on the shoulder as she tucked behind him.

"I got no way to pay my fucking rent now," shouted the redheaded camera guy beside me.

I'm sorry, I almost told him, but any words would have been drowned out by the skull-slapping blast behind us. A burning hand smacked my face. I turned as a crumpled oxygen canister zipped skyward atop a pillar of flame like a cheap rocket, chased by a greasy fireball darkening into black smoke as it clawed for the stratosphere. Bits of smoldering metal rained onto the ground, the Ford's dented roof, our heads.

"Fuck," Barrett hissed, swiping bits of debris from his bare arms.

I worked my jaw as if that would help my eardrums recover from this latest pounding. I couldn't see the side of the shipping container that had absorbed most of the blast, but I assumed from the new crimp in the roof that the wall we'd previously used for cover was a charred ruin. If we'd still been there, the cops would have collected our remains with a mop.

The gunfire had slackened as everyone paused to watch the shed's destruction. Now it resumed, a few crackles and pops that quickly grew into an uninterrupted roar. I even heard the flat boom of a .50-caliber rifle somewhere out there, each shot capable of vaporizing an engine block, and I hoped whoever was behind the scope was on our side, or at least shooting at the people who were shooting at us.

From our new vantage point, I had a clear view of the property's downward slope and the parking lot beyond. In the middle of the lot idled a pickup with a shell over the rear bed, the sun reflecting off metal plates welded over the windows and side panels. It reminded me of the hillbilly armor we used to bolt onto our vehicles in Iraq once the insurgents upgraded their IEDs to punch through standard-issue steel. A robber peeked from behind its hood and fired at the contestants beside the parked cars.

"Who are these guys?" Barrett asked.

"Not a threat to us, I don't think," I said, cringing at a nearby shotgun blast. "They're after the money. If we just stay put . . ."

"Oh, they're not taking our money," Frankie said, shoving her rifle into my hands before scooting forward enough to try the Ford's left-rear door. It creaked open and she slithered into the interior, the car rocking on its springs.

"What the hell are you doing?" I called.

A rattling thump from inside the Ford, followed by Frankie's gleeful shout. The Ford rolled forward a half-foot. "Parking brake is off," she called. "I'm coming back."

I knew what she was about to do. "Everybody behind the trunk," I said.

"What're we doing?" Barrett said, his voice edged with panic—or maybe anticipation. When your ears are ringing thanks to a massive gunfight and a shed blasting into orbit, it's hard to read the nuances of a conversation.

Frankie slithered from the Ford and belly-crawled into our tight scrum, flipped onto her belly and rose to a crouch. "Pushing," she said, taking her rifle back, shouldering it.

I saw her plan. "Not the smartest," I offered, gripping the Ford's bumper.

"But easily the best," she said, and winked. "Now let's move this mother."

Barrett and his buddy threw their shoulders against the angle of the Ford's trunk, braced their feet, and joined me in pushing as hard as they could. The Ford's frame whined and squealed, but the vehicle moved forward—slowly at first. The YouTube guys lowered their equipment and slapped their soft hands on the trunk and pushed, too. The Ford rolled faster.

Frankie crab-walked just behind us, squinting over her sights as she swept for targets.

As the Ford crept past Eric's splattered body, I scooped and collected his fancy rifle. A shot snapped past my cheek. I edged behind the car again. The five robbers had emerged from the house and were working their way toward the parking lot in two squads, not bothering with cover as they sprinted and fired. Three of them had enormous duffel bags on their backs, which slowed them only a little. Whoever these guys were, they were strong, too.

A flurry of shots smashed into the Ford, puncturing the hood and smashing the windshield, but the vehicle's bulk shielded us nicely as it followed the property's natural dip toward the road.

I sighted on the robber trailing his group and fired a short burst. Eric was right: it was a nice rifle with a smooth action, well-balanced as it kicked against my shoulder. I would have given it a great YouTube review.

Beside me, Frankie squeezed off a few rounds towards the parking lot. I followed her sightline. One of the robbers had darted from cover to open the front passenger door of the armored car, crouching beside it as he blazed at a couple of good ol' boys behind a nearby Jeep. At least one of Frankie's shots must have found its mark, because he fell on his ass, his rifle pointing in the air.

I shifted my aim and fired at that guy and missed. The incline steepened beneath us, the Ford speeding up. The YouTube guys broke away, sprinting for new cover behind a truck, while

Barrett and his friend rose and began firing at the robbers who had reached the parking lot. Given the number of people emptying guns at them, I was surprised our new enemies were still upright: their high-end armor could absorb shrapnel and buckshot and maybe a few bullets, but some of the larger rifles should have put them down.

Then again, I'd seen my share of crazy shit that seemingly violated the laws of probability and physics, Humvees driving through explosions untouched and dead-on bullets somehow weaving around their screaming targets. These guys were just lucky—very lucky.

Well, not all of them. Frankie fired again and the guy on the ground twitched and tumbled onto his back, a chunk of his high-tech helmet spinning away.

The remaining robbers plunged through the armored truck's open door. The vehicle peeled away, its exhaust pipe farting black smoke, its engine whining beneath the weight of its armor. Its fat ass fishtailed onto the two-lane, sparking as a few contestants volleyed parting shots.

"We might be in trouble," I said, putting my hand on Frankie's shoulder to stop her as the Ford barreled through the parking lot and crunched hard into the flank of someone's new Cybertruck, crumpling it. There was some metaphor in there about the failures of new technology, but my brain was too exhausted to put it together.

8.

Crazy Bill wandered through the smoking remains of his shooting contest, a bloody hand clutched to the side of his head, moaning, "Robbed . . . robbed . . . robbed . . ."

With the departure of the robbers' armored-up truck, the contestants' wild shooting had trailed off. The air stank of burning metal and gasoline. I spun slowly on my heel, counting bodies: at least nine, although the shed's explosion might have vaporized a few more. I didn't envy the detectives tasked with figuring out who shot who with what.

Speaking of which, we probably needed to leave the scene before the cops arrived.

The other contestants must have been gripped by the same fear of law enforcement, because dozens of them scrambled for their cars and roared away. I imagined more than a few had outstanding warrants for everything from manslaughter to child support. The Cybertruck owner, his cheeks streaked with tears, tried driving his damaged vehicle away from the chaos, only for it to grind to a halt after a few feet, its brake lights flashing spastically.

Barrett and his friend were nowhere to be seen, and I wondered if they'd fled, as well. If so, that was too bad—I was already starting to think of them as friends.

"You want to get out of here?" I asked Frankie.

She shrugged. "Definitely. But first, we need to figure out the chucklefucks responsible for this. They're military, yeah? How they moved. The professionalism."

"That's what I'm guessing. Or they're cops," I said, wiping the trigger guard and stock of Eric's fancy rifle with the hem of my shirt before tossing it in the dust. If the police corralled us, I didn't want any connection with any weapon that might have put rounds in another human being.

"Cops want to think they're military," she said, "but they don't move like that, don't act like that. No, we're dealing with some steely critters here. Oh, good." Slinging her own rifle behind her back, Frankie strode to the robber she'd whacked and knelt beside the body. At least one round had shattered the helmet, but it looked like the kill shot had penetrated through the center of the chest armor and out the back, based on the epic pool of blood darkening the dust beneath him.

Through the shattered visor, a faded blue eye gazed into eternity. Frankie worked loose the chin strap and peeled the helmet off, revealing a sharp-cheeked face with a scraggly blonde beard. The bullet had torn a deep trench through the man's left cheek, the skin around it an ugly purple.

"Recognize him?" she asked.

"No," I said, kneeling beside her. I pulled out my phone and shot his portrait from four angles, then rose and stepped back and snapped a few more photos from a distance. I didn't need to be Sherlock Holmes to see that the guy's gear was standard-issue, available in a thousand gun stores and online. We wouldn't track this crew down through some specialized purchases.

Frankie patted the corpse's pockets. "This dude doesn't have his wallet on him."

"Unsurprising."

She stripped off the guy's elbow pads and rolled up the sleeves. No tattoos. She popped free the guy's armor and pulled up his torn and bloody shirt, exposing a bruised torso punctured with two bloody holes, no more than a quarter inch apart.

"Good shooting, if I do say so myself," Frankie said.

We were starting to draw a crowd. "Whatchu doin'?" someone asked to my left.

"Just looking," Frankie called over her shoulder.

I knelt again and helped Frankie roll the guy onto his side. No tattoos on the guy's torso and back. So much for identifying him that way. I wondered how long until the first cops arrived. Ten minutes? Twenty? No more than that.

"I can send a photo of the guy's face to some people I know," I told her. "Maybe they'll recognize him, but it's a long shot, and I don't have access to any kind of fancy facial databases . . ."

"I think I can solve that." Frankie stood and walked the path connecting the parking lot to the shooting range, stopping beside the torn-up body of a dude in a Spider-Man t-shirt. She bent and lifted the dude's pale arm, revealing the stock of a 12-gauge shotgun tucked beneath his torso. She pulled the weapon free and broke it open to reveal two shells glittering in the sunlight.

"That ain't yours," offered a bystander in a trucker cap.

"Mind your own fucking business," Frankie said, returning to the robber's body.

"Oh no," I said, not because I cared much about her intentions with the corpse, but because my ears were already traumatized from the gunfire and explosions.

"Oh yes," she replied, snapping the shotgun closed and jamming the barrel into the dead robber's right elbow. I jammed my fingers in my ears, not caring if it made me look like a wimp, as she pulled the trigger. The boom was loud enough to make my skull hum and my eardrums snap. The robber's forearm flopped across the gravel like a dying fish.

The crowd shouted and groaned. I offered them a shaky smile and a cheerful wave. "We know what we're doing!" I shouted.

"Shit!" Crazy Bill shouted from somewhere near the house, although it was difficult to tell if he was remarking on Frankie desecrating a corpse, the robbery, or the current state of his life.

Frankie tossed the shotgun aside and gripped the severed limb by the thumb. "Grab me that cooler over there," she said. "The one with the red lid."

The crowd parted to let me grab the cooler from beside a green pickup. As I opened its lid and tossed out the six-pack of cheap beer inside, I wondered if anyone was filming us with their phones. We could leave in the next few minutes and the cops might still track us down. If we were lucky, they'd only charge us with impeding an investigation, doing terrible things to a dead body, whatever.

I dropped the cooler at Frankie's feet, the lid open, and she dropped the limb inside, ice spraying everywhere. "Let's hit the road," she said, slamming the lid closed.

"You can't just go!" a woman yelped.

Crazy Bill appeared, waving his hands in the air, his mouth twisted into a rictus of horror. "You gotta give a statement," he said, his volume reduced from an anguished howl to a loud whine. "You gotta."

"I most assuredly don't," Frankie said, lifting the cooler and tilting her body so Crazy Bill could see the rifle slung on her back, the threat it implied. I had moved ahead of her to the driver's side door of my truck, unlocking it.

"Bill," I said as I opened my door. "We're gonna do our best to find out who did this, okay? That's why we're taking that arm."

"And you'll help get my money back, right?" Crazy Bill whined.

"We'll do our best," Frankie said, opening the back door and tossing the cooler inside. As she slammed the door shut again, I noted she had her fingers of her left hand crossed like a schoolkid.

"And you'll help get my money back, right?" Crazy Bill said again, followed by something else lost as I slid behind the wheel, stabbed my key into the ignition, and roared the engine to life.

I half-expected someone to block our exit, to demand we wait for the cops, but this was Idaho, the land of letting people do whatever the hell they want. I had some trouble reversing out of the space because of the Cybertruck stalled behind me, but once I eased past that high-tech dumpster of a car, I accelerated over the tiny strip of brush separating the lot from the road, then pointed us west. We had a lot of work to do.

9.

Frankie leaned back in her seat and pulled out her phone. "What a shit show, huh? I guess we can stick on this road for a bit, find a way to loop back to Boise."

"We're so unbelievably screwed," I said. My kid, my home, my peace—all of it was gone forever. And then there was the small matter of those FBI guys lurking around and Frankie's insane plan to free our dead friend's kid from the clutches of the most powerful man in the state, not to mention a guy whose death we'd witnessed on a Louisiana highway . . .

My brain was already slapping together the checklist from hell:

We'd have to kill Ivan.

We'd have to run from the FBI.

We'd have to avoid Janine killing us both slowly.

It meant more bodies than I was willing to accept. Except what choice did I have?

"No, we're not," Frankie said, snapping me back to reality. She jerked a thumb over her shoulder at the cooler in the back. "Remember when we used a 3D printer to copy that football player's fingerprints, broke into his phone?"

"Yeah?" Years ago, one of Idaho's richest men had set up a sick game in the backwoods, inviting his fellow millionaires to hunt people for sport, including a student at a local high school who was a football star. Frankie and I had uncovered the plot by unlocking the kid's phone. We killed the millionaires. Good times.

"I got a guy with a scanner and a bunch of cop logins," she said. "If the dead guy's in any database, it'll ring cherries in, like, three seconds."

"Good," I sighed, "because that's all we have to go on."

She slapped me companionably on the shoulder. "Not quite. We could hit all the autobody shops in the area, ask if they weld armor onto trucks for a fee."

"That strikes me as more of a do-it-at-home sort of project. I mean if you want to avoid people talking about it. Or calling the cops." I swallowed. "What if we can't get the money back?"

"We'll hide out until next year," she said, "and then we'll rob Crazy Bill. Those shooting competitions, they clearly have a lot of cash around."

"Somehow I don't think Crazy Bill is going to host that contest again." I sighed and punched the steering wheel. "Fuck. Fuck. Fuck. Fuck. Fuck."

"Bro, relax. Wait, let me take that back: don't relax. But don't totally freak out before you need to. We'll get some fingerprints, then we'll work our way up the chain." Her fingers blurred on her phone's keyboard as she fired off texts, powering up her old network. "In fact, I know something that will take your blood pressure down a few notches: I'm going to call the Monkey Man, have him on standby after we get those prints. I don't care what he's doing or who's paying him, he's coming back into the Frankie fold."

Frankie's bad lieutenant knew how to hurt folks. He'd blown up so many cars and buildings in his time, he could have opened his own demolition firm. "I feel more relaxed already," I said, even though I knew Monkey Man couldn't help with getting the FBI off our backs. And as I knew from my time in the military, nobody brings down the hammer harder than Uncle Sam.

10.

When we looped back toward Boise, Frankie directed me to take an exit off 84 and head into a trailer park behind a used-car lot. I'd spent too much of my life in trailer parks, cuffing people who'd made the dumb decision to skip bail, and entering one always made me a little tense. She had me drive to the lot's back edge and park beside a collapsing chain-link fence. The nearest trailer had a red-and-white paintjob stained with liberal amounts of rust and grime, its roof spiked with antennas.

As we exited my truck, the trailer's door opened and a guy who looked like a two-legged muskrat emerged into the sunlight, all scraggly beard and thick eyeglasses and widely spaced teeth. He waved to Frankie with a bandaged hand.

"Heya, Reaper," Frankie said. "Long time no see."

"I heard you were dead," Reaper said, retreating into his doorway.

"I get that a lot," Frankie replied, fetching the cooler from the back of the truck. "You ready to go to work?"

"If you got the guns."

Frankie stopped. "I said you'd get those later. And my word's still good, right?"

Reaper paused as if thinking it over, then shrugged and gestured for us to follow him inside. Based on the shoddy state of the trailer's exterior, I steeled myself as we stepped through the front door, expecting a hoarder's paradise. Instead, the interior was spotless and minimalist, with four folding chairs and a long set of tables heavy with equipment: hard drives, screens, scanners, printers, and anything else you might need to steal an identity or blackmail someone out of their crypto. Two strings of multicolored Christmas lights gave the scene a cheery glow.

Reaver waved at us to sit while he veered for the stainless-steel fridge in the kitchenette. "Want something to drink?" he asked. "You two look like shit."

"Thanks," Frankie said. "You got any water, we'd appreciate it."

"I assume that's the cooler you texted about, the one with the guy's severed limb in it. You can set it anywhere." Reaper pulled three plastic bottles of water from the fridge and tossed two to us.

"Thanks." Frankie drained her water in one gulp.

Reaper opened a cabinet and pulled out a box of purple surgical gloves and snapped on a pair, then walked over to the cooler and opened it and squinted at the shredded forearm. "You use a saw?" he asked.

Frankie shrugged. "Shotgun. Only thing I had on hand, pun definitely intended."

"I was about to say, your cutting skills really suck." With his free hand, he opened one of the scanners and slapped the limb on it, palm-down. "Don't worry, this'll take just a few minutes."

I opened my bottle, meaning to only take a sip, but when the water touched my lips I was seized by the primal urge to guzzle it all down. I must have lost a gallon of sweat on Crazy Bill's range. While I rehydrated, I watched Reaper open a battered laptop and smack a few keys, awakening the screen.

The scanner hummed. I tried to ignore the blood seeping from beneath the lid and onto the trailer's linoleum flooring. A high-definition image of the dead hand appeared on the screen, and Reaper zoomed in until the screen filled with fingerprint whorls, which he cropped into separate images. As he opened a new series of windows and dragged the images into them, he said, "Frankie, you want to tell me where you got this particular cut of meat?"

"No," Frankie said.

"Okay. I figure I'll hear about it at some point, one way or another." Reaper hit a button and new windows appeared, faces and data scrolling past faster than a hummingbird's blink. He hissed through his teeth.

"Is there a problem?" Frankie asked.

"Depends on you." Reaper clicked his mouse to expand one of those windows to full screen, revealing the bruise-free face of the dead guy alongside a scroll of official-looking information. "Because your guy is a heavy hitter. Or was, I'm guessing. Name's Neal Himes. Former military, 82nd Airborne, plus a bunch of arrests once he got out, but no convictions."

"Arrests for what?" I asked.

"Armed robbery," Reaper said.

"Shocker," Frankie said. "Whatever you're looking at, does it feature an address, known associates, all that good stuff?"

"Yeah." A few more clicks. "His associates are also known badasses, so if they're pissed at you for whatever happened, well, you better buckle up. In any case, I can print all this out for you. Want the limb back?"

Frankie grunted. "I appreciate the offer, but can you get rid of it for me? Otherwise, I'm throwing it in the river or something."

"Sure, the guy down the road's got some fight dogs, I can just toss it to them. Not the first time I've had to get rid of incriminating beef," Reaper said, and winked before shifting his attention to the printer spitting paper at the table's far end.

"We appreciate this," I said.

"I'm gonna appreciate my guns when Frankie delivers," Reaper said, distracted by a new window on his screen. "Oh, hold up. This is cool."

"Cool good," Frankie said, "or cool bad?"

"It's new software I got. Figures out whether somebody's got LLCs, aliases, good stuff like that. Some machine learning algorithm, mapping out the dark web or some shit, I understand it, yeah? But I also don't." He tapped the computer's trackpad and the printer whirred again. "That's for you, too. Guys got a hidden house, from the looks of it. Purchased under a different name."

We'd have to move fast on this info, I knew. The cops would fingerprint the dead guy's remaining hand and access the same databases. Our main advantage was bureaucracy: we might have a day or two, maybe even longer, before an exhausted detective ran the prints and started chasing down addresses. I wanted a coffee, something to recharge my dull nerves, but we'd have to get it from a drive-thru, because I could see Frankie's foot already tap-tap-tapping.

11.

"First stop: this guy's secret house. I bet we find something nefarious there," Frankie said as we rumbled out of the trailer park. She flicked on her phone and input an address from the sheaf of paper that Reaper had printed off. "It's in Meridian, some subdivision."

Meridian was on my way home from Boise, impossible to miss. A few years ago, when Frankie and I had ventured there on a bad bit of business a little too similar to this one, I remembered being dismayed at how the area had changed since my childhood, its fields and spectacular views of the hills replaced by ugly malls and ever-larger houses. The growth had continued unchecked ever since, the last bits of land by the highway exit giving way to shiny apartment buildings that wouldn't have been out of place in Denver.

I wondered how long this growth would last. Something had to give at some point—probably the water supply, considering how many new people were running their showers and watering their endless green lawns. One of my neighbors had built a bunker into the hillside beneath his house, complete with a year's worth of water and food, and although that struck me as mildly insane, he was right about the way this was all headed:

straight into chaos, just like I'd witnessed back in Iraq, a bunch of groups shooting each other apart over religion and politics and basic needs—

I shook my head to snap out of my reverie before I drove us off the road.

When I was overseas, my unit sometimes established the perimeter for Special Forces operators on missions to secure high-value targets. And by 'secure high-value targets,' I mean shooting jihadi ringleaders in the head, which was no big loss for the world—those evil pricks ordered dozens of teenagers to strap on suicide belts and detonate themselves at checkpoints. During those raids, those operators would grab any laptops and papers they found for the intelligence guys back on base. The intelligence guys would sort through the data as quickly as they could and develop new targets.

The Special Forces guys would take that information and go out again, sometimes twice per night. The pace was insane. It was also necessary as we surged troops into Iraq to stabilize a situation our leaders had let go to shit.

Frankie and I, we were on that cadence now. Whatever we found at that robber's hidden house, it would probably lead us somewhere else.

We needed to stay ahead of the cops, stay ahead of these robbers.

God, I was exhausted just thinking about it.

"What's your brilliant plan when we get there?" I asked. "By the way, you need to give me directions now."

She consulted her phone. "Sorry, I'm distracted by Monkey Man not texting me back. Take a right at the next light. As for plans, I'm improvising. At some point, one of the guys on this crew will have to swing around, maybe to destroy evidence, whatever. Then we'll be waiting."

"Cops could also show up."

"True. So maybe we do a quick smash-and-grab, find something tells us who the rest of this crew is."

"I have zero urge to kick in a door, not knowing what's behind it."

"I'm betting you haven't used up all your luck today, despite a million bullets flying at us. Get in the suicide lane up here and bang a left into that entrance."

I followed orders. "What if there's a family in this house?"

"Families don't live in houses owned by aliases or shell corps or whatever. Look, stop being nervous. We'll park down the street for a bit, watch, decide on our next move once we have a good idea of what's going on. Unlike the thing with Anthony's daughter, I bet the FBI isn't watching this house." She shrugged. "Maybe I should have stayed in Mexico."

"I would've kept missing you."

"Aw, you're sweet." She clapped my shoulder. "I'm glad I'm back. I'm just sorry for all this chaos. Take a right, a left, then another right, and the house should be there. We might want to park a little way further down. By the way, you stink."

I pinched my collar and lifted it over my nose. Yep, I smelled like an eye-watering combination of dried sweat, scorched wood, dust, and blood. "You're not exactly daisy-fresh yourself, sis."

"Wrong." She smacked me lightly on the back of the neck. "I smell magical. It's going to be okay, understand? We've gotten through worse."

She wasn't wrong on that front: in our lives, 'worse' had included a gunfight against a dozen guys in a burning field. Holy hell, weren't we entitled to a little peace at some point? A bit of calm to compensate for what had become *decades* of shooting and running?

Sure. The peace and calm of the grave.

Shut up, brain.

I shuddered, which Frankie misinterpreted as the air conditioning cranked too high. She turned it down, and I nodded my thanks, unwilling to kick off a heartfelt conversation with her about our lives. She would just laugh off my concerns like she always did, because she had to be the toughest of us, the smartest, the best.

We worked our way deeper into an older subdivision, its quiet roads lined with ranch houses from another era. Frankie pointed at a tan one on a curve, its windows smeared with years' worth of grime, its yard lined with a white picket fence broken in places like jagged teeth. I drove another hundred yards and parked in the shadow of an ancient tree.

"During the day might not be the best time for this," I said, scanning the surrounding houses for video doorbells, seeing none.

"During the day is the best time," Frankie said. "Everybody's at work. We should have stopped for snacks. I'm so hungry I could eat a live chicken like a circus geek."

"I think there's an old pack of gum in the glove compartment."

"Yeah, but it'll sit in my stomach for seven years." She tilted the rearview mirror for a better angle out the back window. "We'll give it a few minutes, okay, and then we'll go in."

"What if they show up after we're inside?"

"Then we're set up perfectly for an ambush." She squinted and mimed firing a rifle at a spread of targets. "And if that happens, we're taking half the money before we give the rest back to Crazy Bill. Consider it a finder's fee."

"He might object to that."

"Not if we tell him the rest of it burned, or it was lost, whatever."

"I'm not totally comfortable with the idea."

She snorted and shook her head. "Okay, Captain America. But think it over, that's all I ask. Just make it quick because it looks like something's up."

She was hogging the mirror, so I twisted in my seat to see whatever had caught her attention. A gray sedan had swept around the corner, slicing up the quiet road like a shark cruising for prey. It slowed and turned into the tan house's driveway and stopped. On reflex I dipped down while Frankie stayed upright.

A slim man in jeans and a black t-shirt climbed from the driver's seat of the sedan. He was pale, with a hawklike nose and close-cropped red hair and long sideburns that almost reached his jawline. He shut the door behind him and locked it and opened the trunk and pulled out two duffel bags and set them on the driveway and closed the trunk again. He paused and closed his eyes and rolled his neck—something about that last gesture seemed familiar, but I couldn't quite put my finger on it.

"Shit," Frankie breathed.

"What?" I asked.

The man picked up the duffel bags again and walked up the driveway. He seemed to struggle a little under the weight. It was too far to see whether the bags were dusty, but they looked quite a bit like the ones we'd seen the robbers throwing into their armored car at Crazy Bill's range. He disappeared inside the house.

Frankie pulled out her phone and dialed a number. When someone answered, she said, "Hey, I was wondering if you wanted to get together, talk over some stuff. What are you up to?"

She paused to listen; her brow furrowed.

"No, that's okay," she said, "I'll catch you when you're back in town."

She ended the call and jammed the phone into her pocket like she was stuffing her worst enemy's head into a toilet.

"What was that about?" I asked.

Her hands curled into fists, tight enough for her knuckles to strain against the skin. Her fury crackled in the car's hot atmosphere like lightning. "That guy who just walked in there?" she said. "That was Monkey Man. You didn't recognize him without the mask. He's the one who has our fucking money."

"You just called him?"

"Yeah, and *he lied to me*." Her voice dissolved into a hiss. Her eyes were wide, wild. "No, it's even worse than that. I told him I was shooting in that contest, and he went and robbed it anyway. What kind of backstabbing bitch does that?"

12.

F rankie drew her pistol. "We're going in," she said.

"And do what?" I asked. "Kill him?"

I wondered whether Frankie, despite her skills, could win against her bad lieutenant in a fight. In a state full of crazy killers and gunslingers, Monkey Man was feared for good reason: he was quicker than Doc Holliday on the draw, crazier than a rabid animal cornered beneath a house. A long time ago, a local ruffian named Zombie Bill had stolen a pair of AR-15s from me, and that situation escalating out of hand had led to Monkey Man blowing him up with a rocket launcher—more than enough to cement his status as someone you didn't cross.

Of course, Monkey Man might hesitate when facing down Frankie. Their bond ran deep.

Then again, he hadn't worked for Frankie for a long time. Maybe he hated her now, or he'd decided to make a break with his old life. Maybe that's why he wasn't wearing his famous mask anymore.

"What's his real name?" I asked.

Her brow scrunched in confusion. "What?"

"I'm curious. What's his real name?"

Her anger seemed to cool a few degrees. "Jimmy," she said, slipping her pistol into its holster.

"Maybe he did it for a good reason," I said, pleased with myself as she leaned back in her seat and exhaled. The underworld might have feared my sister, but I'd always known how to talk to her, which buttons to press to calm her down. I should have been a shrink, maybe—

"Fuck it," Frankie said, kicking open her door, and climbed out before I could grab her shoulder. By the time I opened my own door to follow her, she was halfway down the block, walking fast, tucking her shirt over her holster. I had to shift back into combat mode. We had no idea how many people might be waiting inside. If we wanted a chance at survival we needed to think tactically about entrances and how to clear rooms.

"Wait—" I hissed, reaching for her as she strode up the driveway.

"Fuck it," Frankie said, louder, and slapped my hand away. Drawing her pistol, fired off two shots into the lock before ramming her foot against it. As the door shook open, she ducked slightly and darted to the right, disappearing into the blackened interior.

It had been a long time since I'd needed to kick in a door or clear a house. They say that you never lose muscle memory, that you'll always know how to sidestep the fatal funnel and slice a room, but as I sprinted toward the door after Frankie I felt too awkward, too stiff, my movements almost out of control. I fumbled out my gun and tucked it tight against my body in case a lurking opponent on the other side of the doorway tried to grab it.

No shots from inside the house.

I slipped through the doorway as quickly as I could, into the dark and the cool. It stank of mildew. After the blazing sunlight outside, my eyes struggled to adjust, and I caught a blued square of window to my right, the dim outlines of furniture, the black lumps of the bags that Monkey Man had carried inside, the paler blur of Frankie disappearing through yet another doorway ahead.

"Behind," I shouted, hoping that wouldn't draw fire from anyone. In a cheap house like this one, its insides slapped together from spit and drywall, it would be easy enough for someone with a high-powered weapon to fire through a wall.

From the doorway in front of me, Frankie yelled, *"Stop."*

I entered the next room, which was long and narrow with a large window at the far end overlooking a yard overgrown with dry brush. If you put a sizable table in the middle, it might have served as a good dining room. Frankie stood to the left of the doorway, her pistol pointed at Monkey Man—Jimmy—who stood at the far end, his arms raised slightly. He was fifteen feet away, close enough to charge at us and maybe get lucky.

Frankie must have realized that, because her finger was tight on the trigger, no more than a half-ounce away from firing. I stepped to the right and aimed my own gun at Jimmy's head.

Jimmy lowered his hands. "I saw you down the street," he said, his voice clipped, lightly accented. I'd heard it before, once, after Frankie was shot. "You didn't need to kick in the door like that."

I wondered whether he had a weapon tucked into his waistband beneath his loose t-shirt. I had no urge to search him. This was a guy who wore a monkey mask and blew things up for fun. He probably had pockets full of blades.

"Yeah, I could've just rung the bell?" Frankie said. "You'd better start talking, bud."

"I'd never hurt you."

Frankie snorted. "Yeah? I'm sorry, I must be confused. Did you not just rob that shooting contest? Did you not fire at me?"

Jimmy shook his head. "No," he said, louder. "We waited until you left the course. The men had strict orders not to fire at you. We were focused on clearing the house and taking the money, not killing any contestants."

"Where are the other men?" I asked.

"They are coming," Jimmy said. "And soon. You had better leave."

"How much is in the bags?" Frankie asked.

"In the ones I brought in? More than a million," Jimmy said, almost whispering. "What did you expect me to do?"

Frankie's gun wavered. "What?"

"When you left for Mexico. I had to get paid. Had to live. Had to find," he swallowed, "a new patron, I suppose you could say."

"Who's your patron?" I asked, a part of me already realizing the answer—and dreading it.

"It's Deacon Dunn, that gunrunner wannabe, isn't it?" Frankie asked. "If it wasn't, whoever you're working for would have sent you after him at some point—and, well, he's still alive."

Jimmy offered us a tight-lipped smile and nodded slightly. "Yes. He's not you, Frankie, but he's good at what he does. Very good. He also needs cash for a very big plan, which is why he ordered us to take down that contest."

Engines roared outside, along with the squeal of rubber on pavement. Keeping my pistol on Jimmy, I stepped to the doorway and glanced to my right, through the kitchen windows overlooking the street. I was thinking maybe the cops put the clues together in record time, but we weren't that lucky: the two trucks screeching to a halt by the curb were battered, dusty, and loaded with hard-looking men. A moment later, a sleek BMW SUV slid up the driveway.

"That's him, I'm guessing," Jimmy said.

The BMW stopped. I zeroed on the hulking silhouette behind the wheel.

"We should go out the back," I said. "Does the yard have a gate?"

"Fuck that," Frankie said, marching toward Jimmy with her gun raised. "We're exiting through the damn front, and you're going to help us do it."

I took another wide step to the right, trying to keep Jimmy covered as Frankie approached, just in case he tried to draw down or disarm her, but he remained passive as a tranquilized lamb while she gripped his collar and spun him around, her pistol pressed to the back of his head.

"I'm not sure he values my life that much," Jimmy said. "Or anyone's, for that matter."

"Well, maybe he'll figure your body will absorb the first bullets," she said, patting him down, "give me too much time to get that first shot off. Where's your gun?"

She found it tucked into his waistband, a small black pistol that might have been a .25, but it was hard to tell in the dark. Tossing it aside, she patted his pockets, paused on his left hip, and grunted.

"Careful," Jimmy said.

"I knew you were holding out on me, you little firebug." Grinning Frankie pulled a small black sphere from his pocket. "These are hard to find. What'd you do, rob an Army depot?"

"Friend in the SEALS," Jimmy said. "Brought it back from overseas. Gave it to me for . . . services rendered. Something larger wouldn't fit in my pants."

"There's an easy joke in there, but we're short on time." Frankie tossed the sphere to me. "It's a mini-frag, Special Forces issue. They stopped manufacturing them, like thirty years ago. Let's move."

The sphere was heavy for its size. I kept it in my left hand, my thumb through the metal ring on the pin, as I pressed myself against the nearest wall, giving Frankie and Jimmy plenty of space to exit into the front room. As they passed, I stepped behind them, positioning myself a half-step to Frankie's left. The busted front door creaked open, revealing a bearded man in sunglasses and camouflage, a silver pistol pressed against his thigh. He regarded us silently before ducking out of sight again.

Frankie stopped, her breathing loud in the gloom. I was doing my best to keep an eye on the front door and the windows to my left and right. Part of me wanted to scoop up one of the duffel bags beside the couch, loaded with enough money to solve all our problems, but I knew the weight was too much if we wanted to move fast.

If we lived past the next minute, that was.

I gripped the grenade tighter in my sweaty palm, wondering if I should pull the pin. It would give us an advantage if I was smart about it.

"Frankie," announced a loud, cheerful voice from outside. "I'm Deacon Dunn. I have no interest in killing you, understand?"

Frankie stayed silent.

"I'm coming in," Dunn said. "You don't fire, you stay alive. You fire, we'll kill you and your brother, then the rest of your family, then your friends. Understood?"

I looked at Frankie, who shrugged.

"Just you come in," Frankie called. "And you walk in slowly, no jacket, no gun, understood?"

"Fine. Coming in now." Dunn stepped into the doorway. He wasn't what I expected: large enough to be a former footballer, his Viking beard neatly trimmed, the sides of his skull shaved almost clean. He wore a sport jacket tailored to his muscled frame, along with an expensive shirt and a pair of pressed slacks. He could have been one of those hipster barbers who charged fifty bucks downtown for a shave and a haircut, or a startup guy who'd decided that Silicon Valley was a little too liberal and Boise was his kind of town.

Except those guys didn't scare me. Something about Dunn reminded me of guys who joined the military because they wanted to kill, guys who ended up in prison later for shooting or knifing prisoners because they hungered for blood on their hands. Guys who seemed more like sharks than people.

"Not gonna lie, I admire you. You're a legend in your own lifetime," Dunn said, seeming like he meant it. He stripped off his jacket and hung it on the ruined doorknob, then rotated so we could see that his waistband was gun-free. "I think we'll have a lot to discuss. A lot of common ground. If you want to stop pointing that gun at me, I think there's still some decent beer in that fridge over there. What do you say?"

13.

This guy was going to kill us. The big question was whether he wanted to do it now, by lulling us under the guise of a chat before having his men bushwhack us, or later, once we'd left and our guard was down. I suspected the latter: why risk a close-quarters gunfight with someone like Frankie when he could snipe us in my driveway tomorrow night?

I wasn't taking any chances. As Dunn entered the house, I popped the pin on the mini-grenade and held it over the duffel bags, my thumb pressing the handle in place. With my other hand, I kept my pistol aimed between Dunn's eyes.

I wanted to end him now.

He was too dangerous to let live.

But if he died here, it would mean our end, too.

Dunn paused on the threshold, his eyes flicking from me to the bags. "Okay," he said. "If that's how you want to play it."

"Insurance," I said.

"Like I said, I'm just here to chat," he said, holding up his hands at shoulder height, sidestepping slowly across the room toward the fridge. There might have been a gun in there—I'd brought down more than one criminal who thought storing a pistol in the vegetable bin was a good idea—but I was betting he wouldn't try to use it, not with the prospect of all his money blown to confetti if I dropped the grenade.

Frankie took a step back, swiveling Jimmy so his body would shield her from Dunn and anyone trying to shoot through the doorway.

Dunn opened the refrigerator slowly, standing aside so we could see the four cans of lite beer on the shelves and nothing else. He removed one. "Any of you want to partake?" he asked.

"No," Frankie said. "Jimmy doesn't, either."

I shook my head. "I'm good," I said, keeping my pistol aimed roughly between Dunn and the door.

"Your loss," Dunn said, shutting the fridge door and popping the beer open. Leaning against the kitchen counter, he took a long pull before setting the can on the counter.

"You have quite the reputation," Frankie said. "And I'd love to talk management techniques, payroll tips, all that good criminal mastermind shit, but we're on a bit of a deadline here, so we're just going to take our share of cash out of those bags and walk away, sound good?"

"You put a bet on the match?" Dunn asked.

"Yep, two hundred fifty grand," she lied, "and I was on track to win the whole enchilada before your guys decided to shoot up a shooting contest. Big points for balls, by the way." Her eyes flicked toward me. "Bro, pick up the bags."

Something flickered at the edge of my vision: one of Dunn's guys poking his head around the doorway. I raised the grenade and he disappeared. Kneeling, I unzipped one of the duffel bags with my free hand and opened it, revealing a loose thicket of bills of all sizes, some crumpled and stained.

I remembered my father clapping his rough hand on the back of my neck when I was a little kid. When he bent close, he smelled faintly of beer and that cheap aftershave he loved, the stuff that came in the little bottle with the beach ball on it. *Always do the right thing*, he told me. *Even if it costs you.*

In the end, doing the right thing had cost him everything.

It had cost me everything.

In the truck, I told Frankie I hadn't been comfortable with the idea of taking all the money. I had no such issues now. Maybe later I would feel sorry for those other shooting contestants and their friends who'd put down bets in good faith, thinking they'd win, but this was a matter of pure survival. Frankie had been right before: without money—a lot of money, all the money—we wouldn't have peace. Our family wouldn't have peace.

And our small bit of peace was worth anything.

I stuffed my pistol in my waistband, knelt, and shouldered both bags. My spine bent painfully beneath the weight. It was fifty yards to my truck with a lot of guns pointed at me. How would I manage to carry the money, juggle the grenade, and watch Frankie's back? What if Jimmy tried something ridiculous?

Dunn sighed and rubbed his eyes, like he was an elementary school teacher dealing with a particularly dull student. "You're not taking all of it," he said. "I was willing to tolerate you taking what's yours . . ."

"No, you weren't," Frankie said. "Where you from? You got an accent."

Dunn shook his head and offered us the sunniest fake smile this side of the Mississippi. "I'm from California, and you're not distracting my ass. I'll make you the deal of the century: you leave those bags and walk out of here, and we'll let you go. Consider it a favor to your old lieutenant there."

The edge of Frankie's mouth twitched into a slight grin, the same one she sometimes deployed before she did something crazy. "Nah, we're taking all of it," she said, and her voice was high, light, almost a laugh. "We're dead either way, right, Encino Man?"

"It's Huntington Beach," Dunn snapped. "I came up rougher than you can ever imagine."

"Somehow I doubt that," I said. "They grow us tough out here."

"Okay." Dunn's smile had disappeared. He raised a hand, palm out, before lowering it again. Nodded to himself. "Okay. I get it. Listen to me: we need that money because we're planning something big. Something that's going to bring the power back to the people. You can understand that, right, being from Idaho? Being part of something larger than yourselves?"

"We're not all fucking *militiamen*, your dumbass," Frankie said.

"We're just in it for ourselves," I said, taking a step forward, the bags digging into the soft meat of my shoulders. My back flexed like a rickety wooden bridge in a hurricane. Holy hell, I should have spent the past few years working out harder. I'd lost way too much muscle mass since my military time.

"God spare us from Californication," Frankie said, retreating toward the door, her hand tight on Jimmy's neck. "You ready, bro?"

"Yep," I said.

"Like you're the originals to this land, all high and mighty." Dunn stood tall, his voice rising to a shout: *"How many Native Americans did your granddaddy kill?"*

Jimmy was relaxed in Frankie's grip, his eyes half-lidded, as if he was hanging out on a boat instead of standing at the nexus of too many guns. I expected nothing less from him. Was he crazy enough to try something, though?

I moved as fast as I could toward the door, sweat already pouring from my armpits, the grenade and pistol slippery in my grip. Frankie exited the house first, jerking Jimmy left and right, and as I followed her I saw that Dunn's men had taken position behind their vehicles, aiming pistols and rifles at us. They seemed calm. For now.

Maybe it was because the sun had transformed the outdoors into an oven or maybe it was because I was trying to move with a backbreaking amount of weight, but my shirt was soaked through with sweat in seconds. I could feel it dripping down my legs.

"We have a grenade," Frankie said. "We'll blow the money up."

Their aim remained steady, their eyes cold. They might as well have been robots.

By the time we reached my truck, Dunn had emerged onto the driveway, his hands on his hips. He seemed more amused than anything else, his head cocked slightly. For a quarter-second I considered throwing the grenade to scatter them, except I wasn't the kind of guy to turn a suburban street into Baghdad.

Opening the truck's rear door, Frankie shoved Jimmy inside and climbed after him. I opened my own door and shoved the duffel bags into the front passenger seat as I climbed inside, then twisted the engine to life, expecting the rear window to shatter under a storm of bullets, or maybe a perfectly centered shot would just snap everything to black—

The engine roared and I slammed on the gas and peeled away, still holding the fucking grenade in my left hand. My rearview mirror framed Dunn and his men in the street.

"Bro," Frankie laughed. "Why don't you toss that thing at the nearest gas station?"

"We gotta get Janine," I said. The adrenaline was starting to fade, my hands shaking on the wheel. "We gotta get my kid."

"I ought to kill you," Frankie told Jimmy, grinding the pistol's barrel into his neck. "Dump you out before we hit the highway."

Jimmy shrugged. "I wouldn't blame you."

Frankie laughed. "I knew we still had a level."

The traffic light at the subdivision's exit was red. I ran it, banging a rubber-burning left in the suicide lane, calculating it was three minutes to the highway and another forty minutes to home if the highway wasn't clogged. We could pick up Janine and the guns from the safe and whatever else we might need, and then . . .

What?

We'd grab the kid and then . . .

Flee. But where?

"Back in the house, what did your new boss mean by something big?" Frankie asked. "Something you were planning for?"

Jimmy shrugged. "No idea."

"Liar," Frankie said. "Give me a little hint."

"No," Jimmy said. "I held your secrets. I hold his, too."

"Honorable," I offered.

Jimmy's eyes met mine in the rearview mirror. "I always had a lot of respect for you. I'm sorry it turned out this way."

"You're stalling," Frankie said, jabbing the pistol into Jimmy's knee. She did it softly, though, and I wondered if her anger against him was starting to cool. How long can you stay furious against someone who'd saved your life again and again? In Frankie's case, I felt the answer was "forever," but she'd surprised me before.

"I will say this about Dunn," Jimmy said. "He's not your ordinary criminal. Made a fortune in crypto and drugs before moving here. And he hates the federal government very much."

"Like half the folks in Idaho," I said. The highway ramp was just ahead. I took it at unsafe speed, my tires squealing. "At least on the hate-the-government part."

"He's not your typical sovereign citizen type," Jimmy said. "No, he's got a tech background. He thinks the government should be replaced with 'something small,' as he likes to say. 'We got to balance out the power.'"

"Which means blowing something up," Frankie said. "But what?"

"You can shoot off my leg," Jimmy said, "but you're not getting anything else out of me. It doesn't matter who I'm working for, I never talk."

I shifted lanes, the truck swaying, Frankie's pistol lifting away from Jimmy's leg. "That's what I've always loved about you," she said quietly. "Bro, pull over."

I obeyed. This section of highway ran along a slight rise, offering a panoramic view of the fields giving way to car dealerships and gas stations. I knew Frankie dismissed people living normal lives as cattle sleepwalking through their existences, but a life where my biggest problem was the mortgage seemed pretty good right now.

"Get out. You're getting off lucky. Consider it a favor for all the time we spent together." With that, Frankie shoved him into the burning day and shut the door. As I accelerated back into traffic, she leaned back in her seat, exhaling loudly.

"How long until he tells those guys which way we went?" I asked.

"I hope he won't, for old time's sake, but that's the naïve part of me talking. I'll bet we don't have much time. Very carefully hand me that grenade," she said. "There's a paper clip back here, I can put it in as a pin."

Without taking my eyes off the road, I passed the grenade over my shoulder, not loosening my grip until I felt her finger pressing hard on the safety lever. "We need a plan," I said.

"Oh, I got one." Plucking a paperclip from the back seat, she straightened it with her teeth and slipped the tip through the tiny hole at the base of the pin, fixing it to the grenade. "We have a lot of money in those bags. We're all going to Mexico, starting a new life as a family. We can buy a big hacienda somewhere, live like queens and kings."

Traffic wasn't terrible, and I estimated it would take us maybe forty minutes to get home. With Frankie holding the grenade, I could pull out my phone and tap out a text message to Janine that I dreaded to send: 'GO TO S'S.'

'S'S' stood for Sandy's, a coffee shop near our house that hadn't updated its décor since the Eisenhower administration. It served okay coffee to an audience of truckers and farmers, and I'd always appreciated the Stones-only jukebox in the corner. It was also the designated meetup place for me and Janine if the proverbial cow patty ever hit the fan.

With the text sent, I tossed the phone on top of the duffel bags in the passenger seat. "There's just one little problem," I said. "Didn't you have to flee Mexico because the FBI was crawling up your ass?"

"Yeah, we're going to save Anthony's kid on the way out. Square everything with Anthony's ghost and the FBI. Janine can grab Kelly. Then we all keep driving south."

I punched the wheel.

"Look, bro," she said, "if there's any comfort, you had no choice. You can get someone to sell the house when we're gone. I'll show you how to route the money so nobody can trace it." She leaned forward and squeezed my shoulder. "There are good schools for my darling niece in Mexico. We'll get her in one under a new name. You and I, we can find a company down there, run security, it'll be lucrative . . ."

I swiped her hand away. "I'm not a fugitive. I hunt them, remember?"

She snorted. "You used to. But what do you do now, pick up hours at a gun range? Hope the government won't fuck somehow with your pension and healthcare? A part of you knows this is the best move. That's why you took all the money back there with Dunn."

"I figured it would give us more leverage," I said. "Something's bothering me."

"Understatement of the century. *Everything* is bothering me right now."

"No, what Dunn said. About planning something big. Maybe blowing something up."

Frankie sighed. "And?"

"We can't let that happen. People will die."

She stared out the window at the sun-scorched landscape. "People die every day. I don't see how that's our problem. Especially given our problems right now. Put on your own oxygen mask before helping others, all that shit."

"We can do something. We don't have to be heroes, but we can do something."

"When I first got back here, I thought I could build it back, stronger than ever before," Frankie murmuring like she hadn't heard me, her faint reflection in the glass like a crescent moon over the bright desert. "But now I know I don't have it in me anymore. The old version of me, she would have shot Jimmy by the side of the road, left his corpse as a warning. I don't have the people, either. What's a queen without people?"

"Dunn's got the people."

"Fucking Californians taking everything." She shook her head. "Let's get Janine and get out of here. Mexico, baby!" She laughed, but her eyes were cold and scared.

14.

When we pulled into Sandy's gravel parking lot, I spied Janine through the coffee shop's dusty front window. She had taken the corner booth furthest away from the front door, her back to the wall. She offered me a thumbs-up, which I returned before reversing into a parking spot that gave us a direct shot to the road.

"Want me to come in with you?" Frankie asked.

"No, keep watch out here," I said, cutting the engine as I scanned the area. I recognized the battered Datsun that belonged to Samin and Jill, the couple who ran the shop during the day. Janine's Subaru was on the far side of the building, out of immediate sight of anyone coming from the west—it wasn't much, but at least my wife had picked up enough of my paranoia over the years to park in the most invisible spot. There was only one other car in the lot, one of those brand-new Jeep SUVs, which meant at least one other person inside.

"It'll be okay," Frankie said.

"If she tears my head off my body, just take the truck and head to Mexico."

"Don't make me say 'it'll be okay' again, because I'm not used to being the voice of comfort here. She's not going to tear your head off."

"You've met her, yes?"

"Yes, and yes, she has a temper, and yes, she's often sick of your bullshit." She placed a cold hand on my bicep, fingers clenching like a vise. Maybe she meant the gesture as a friendly one, but it hurt like a bitch. "But, bro, when you've been with someone forever, when you've had a kid with them, when you've been shot at together, that's not a bond that breaks. Not completely. No matter how hard you try."

"She's divorced me before."

"And yet she's here, waiting for you. Is the shit we're in the worst shit we've ever been in? The answer to that question is 'probably yes.'" She gripped harder, her fingernails digging into my flesh, her eyes a little manic. "And there's opportunity here, don't forget. She might dig the idea of a new life in a new place."

"She might not want to go to Mexico, and I wouldn't blame her." I tried to flex my legs, place a hand on the door handle, but my muscles refused to cooperate. I might as well have been rooted to my seat like a tree.

"Well, you better hash that out. She's waiting." She released my arm, reached across my waist, and pulled my door handle. The door cracked open, the day's heat seeping inside. I placed my hand on the frame, thinking of all the times I'd kicked in a door to the unknown. Walking into that coffee shop felt scarier than taking down a Ba'ath safehouse in Baghdad, but Janine was still staring at me through the window, and I didn't want to keep her waiting on top of everything else.

My legs reactivated. The coffee shop's door had a little bell that tinkled as I entered. Samin and Jill paced behind the counter, prepping coffee for a swarthy guy in gray coveralls. They had the jukebox cranked a little too loud, which was great—I didn't need any eavesdroppers. Janine tap-tap-tapped the rim of her full cup of coffee as I approached.

Sliding onto the bench across from her, I noted the black backpack resting against her hip: her go-bag with medications, a metal bottle of water, a hundred dollars in folding cash, a change of underwear, a small first aid kit, and a pistol with extra magazines.

"Hey," I said.

"Hey," she said, her voice flat.

I waited for her to say something, but she was expecting me to fill the void. I swallowed hard and said, "I was trying to do the right thing." And then, before my tongue could freeze up, I poured out the whole mess, every bad decision and bloody detail.

They say confession is good for the soul, but I didn't feel cleansed when I finished.

Janine had stopped tapping her cup. Her face was still as a statue.

"I'm sorry," I said.

"You should have told me," she said, so quietly it was hard to hear her over the music.

"I know. That's the thing I'm sorriest about." I reached halfway across the table, my palm up, hoping against hope she would take my hand.

"I can handle bad news. God knows we've had enough of that over the past few years." She spoke a little louder. I wondered if she was priming to snap.

"I know."

"What's the plan now? If we can't go back to the house."

I glanced out the window at my truck, Frankie a wavering shadow beyond the windshield. "She wants to go to Mexico. We have enough money to start a new life, I guess. If that's what we want."

She stretched out her hand, her fingers a few inches from mine. "And how long do we live that new life before someone tracks us down? A year? Two, if we're lucky?"

"We're tough. We'd make it."

She shook her head. "It's not a plan. Our little girl isn't growing up as a fugitive, you understand?" Her hand snapped into a fist, but her voice was steady. "You're going to fix this, and you're going to fix this here, because this is our home, and nothing runs us off. You try to leave, and we're not coming with you."

"Okay." What else could I say?

"Okay." Her fist loosened, her fingers finding mine and squeezing. "Can I make a suggestion?"

I felt my existence balanced on a knife's edge. Explaining things to Janine hadn't gone as badly as I'd feared, but there was still so much opportunity for things to go wrong.

"You said the FBI will owe you if you deliver that girl," she said, quieter now. "Assuming they're not lying to you and Frankie, you think you can leverage that against all those other fucks who want you dead?"

15.

S tanding in the parking lot beside my truck, Frankie rolled her eyes and said, "That's the dumbest idea I've ever heard. You can't trust a Fed to attack the people you want. They attack who they want to attack."

"There's got to be a way to work it," I said. "You let them take down a bunch of criminal rednecks before they can do some terrorist shit? They love looking good to their bosses."

"Just as long as they forget about us afterwards," Janine said. "Look, here's my idea: I drive away. Grab the kid. Take her someplace even you don't know. You call me when it's over."

It made sense: there were too many people involved in this bloody affair who would cheerfully chop off my toes until I confessed where Janine was hiding my daughter, and then they'd use my family as leverage to get what they wanted. In the meantime, Janine could take care of herself—she'd killed before.

"I still think it's time for Mexico," Frankie said. "Who doesn't like a fresh start?"

Janine raised her hand. "I like my life here just fine."

I had some doubts about that, considering our debts and her stress levels, but wisely chose to keep my mouth shut.

"We have tons of money. We'd live like kings and queens," Frankie said. Did I detect a note of pleading in her voice?

"It's no life for my daughter," Janine said. "It's no life for us. We're not . . . fugitives, no offense."

"None taken," Frankie said, something flickering in her eyes almost too quick to catch. I remembered the night she'd left for Mexico, after taking a bullet to the chest and almost dying, and how standing in the moonlight bathing a quack doctor's dooryard she'd seemed brittle, ancient. Did she expect to die of old age? Did I?

Maybe not, but Janine and my kid were going to have full lives, even if it cost me mine.

"I'm agreeing with Janine here," I said, and it was hard to meet my sister's eyes. "We solve this here."

"And I get out of the blast zone," Janine said. "Keep the kid safe. Because that's ultimately what matters, right? Her safety? Her future?"

Frankie sighed and said, "Shit, okay. Let's play all this on the hard option." Opening the truck's rear door, she unzipped one of the duffel bags in the footwell, plucked out a few bundles of cash, and extended them to Janine. "Take this. With what's left over, you could probably put my niece through college."

"You have no idea how much college is gonna cost," Janine said, slipping the cash into the rear pockets of her jeans. Turning to me, she placed a warm hand on my cheek and said, in her tried-and-true parody of a husky whisper: "Don't you ever hide things from me again."

"Okay," I said, relief flooding me in a warm wave, loosening all my clenched muscles. "Yes."

"And don't get killed," Janine said, before spinning on her heel and retreating across the lot toward her car. It might have seemed cold, her leaving so quickly after a line like that, but I knew she didn't want us to see her tears, didn't want her fear to shake us. I would always love that woman.

I waved to Janine as she steered the Subaru onto the road, but she didn't wave back, just stared into the distance where our daughter waited. Once her car was a shining speck on the horizon, Frankie said, "Here's the plan: we grab the kid. We leverage her to sic the FBI on Dunn and the governor and everyone else who might want to hurt us. We give a chunk of the money back to the contest, so no yahoo gets tempted to track us down and kill us later. We keep the rest, you pay off Ivan, I buy myself a sweet watch and a car. Simple, right?"

"No."

She slapped me on the shoulder. "Glad you agree. Not like you had a choice."

The sun prickled my scalp, sweat cooling as it trickled between my shoulder blades and down the small of my back. Our chances of survival sucked, but like Frankie just said, what options did we have? I'd harbored so many delusions of living a quiet existence in the country. Instead, my life was just kicking down doors again and again, facing death behind each one of them.

16.

Under ordinary circumstances, you wouldn't knock down a door until you had spent several hours or even days watching the target house. You'd note all the doors and windows, try to get a sense of the interior. When I was a bounty hunter, real-estate websites where you could look up the floor plans for an address, along with photos of each room, were my best friend.

I loved double-wides with their factory-standard layouts. I hated double-wides because of their small size: someone could stand in the bedroom or bathroom doorway with a 12-gauge and fill the space with buckshot. Near the end of my career, I'd developed a never-fail technique where I'd run a garden hose from the exhaust pipe of my running truck into any gap or window in the trailer's side, gas the inside until the target crashed into daylight, coughing and gasping.

I always made sure the target was alone when I did that—don't think I'm kind of guy who'll suffocate a kid or a pet.

This thing with Barnes and the girl was the furthest thing from ordinary circumstances. Most of the people I'd cuffed while bounty hunting were losers, freaks who'd failed anger management, and dangerous in their own way—but they weren't trained killers. Hitting this house with Barnes inside would be closer to what I did in Iraq, where you had precious little idea of what awaited you on the far side of the door except a bunch of dudes with Kalashnikovs and suicide vests, dudes who were willing to die if it meant taking you with them.

"I just wish we had more time," I told Frankie as we steered toward Boise. "We're not prepped."

"Oh, ye of little faith," Frankie said, pulling out her phone. "I have a fantastic plan."

"Whenever you use the word 'fantastic,' it scares me."

"Just drive. The shit's hitting the fan, but I don't think we've splattered the whole room quite yet."

I wished I'd gotten a cup of coffee when meeting with Janine. I was wide awake but exhausted, my muscles like warm taffy. It was late afternoon, which meant the arteries into Boise were thickening with traffic, and as we crawled behind an 18-wheeler I had to resist checking my watch and tapping on the wheel. By the time we reached the North End, the western sky was purpling like a fresh bruise, the trees throwing toothy shadows as I rumbled along the quiet blocks.

As much as I wanted to wait for full dark for any kind of smash-and-grab, that would take another five hours at this time of year. At an intersection three blocks away from the target house, I spotted the FBI guys' car on my left, parked beside a set of bungalows half-cloaked by hedges dried almost orange by the sun. The early twilight reflecting off the windshield reduced agents Simmons and Croal to silhouettes. Neither made a move as I rolled past, although I assumed they'd recognized my truck.

"Think they'll be a problem?" I asked.

"Oh yeah, totally, but hopefully more of a problem for other people," Frankie said, distracted by an app open on her phone. "I'm doing pizza. It's only fifteen-minute delivery."

"What?"

"It's not for us, silly. It's so that a pizza guy shows up at their front door to distract while we go in the back. This app, it's got a Track Your Pizza feature, you can see it moving toward you on the map, God bless America."

"I think I saw the delivery-guy tactic in a movie once. I don't think it ended well."

"Well, it'll work in real life, because we're more badass than any stupid movie character. We're going with pepperoni because why not." She tapped a few buttons and nodded to herself before sliding her phone into her pocket again. "You ready?"

"No."

"Amazing. Here we go."

I passed the target house—the windows were dark, the blinds pulled—and took a right. Nobody had built houses on the far side of the block, so we had a clear view of the worn wooden fence, maybe seven feet high, that circuited the house's back yard. The narrow door in the fence had a latch with no lock on it, which struck me as an unforced error. I drove another block and parked beyond a thick patch of dry scrub.

Frankie checked her phone again. "Pizza guy is pulling up. Go, go, go."

"Fuck," I said, kicking open my door.

We crouched as we trotted down the block, drew our pistols as we approached the rear of the house. I scanned the nearby houses for any sign of lights or movement. Nothing. I imagined most people weren't home from work yet, but if this turned into a firefight, the sound would carry far enough to attract our FBI pals.

Or worse, some good citizen would call the cops.

When we reached the fence, I raised a hand for Frankie to pause, then carefully pressed down on the latch and eased the gate open an inch.

I didn't see any taut wires in the gap.

I opened the door a little wider and peered around, leery of dogs and cameras. There was a garden plot to my left, overgrown with browning corn and weeds; the rest of the lawn was spotted with sun-bleached kiddie toys and a picnic bench with cracking planks. I couldn't see any cameras attached to the house's pale flank, and the rear windows were curtained.

Frankie poked me in the back. "Move, soldier."

I sprinted low toward the back door and took a position on the left side of the frame. What was my best move here? We'd been lucky so far but a guy like Percy would keep all the doors locked, maybe alarmed, and—

I twisted the doorknob as quietly as I could, and to my enormous surprise the door popped open. Was this a trap? I slotted my foot into the gap, intending to ease the door wider, my finger tight on my trigger. It was never easy to clear a house, and I'd always opted for slicing a room carefully before moving in—

"*Move*, damnit," Frankie said, shoving past me, knocking the door open with her shoulder as she charged into the house with her gun raised. I followed, panicked, ready for a bullet to knock her out of her boots. The doorway opened onto a small landing and a short flight of wooden steps leading up to a narrow kitchen with a marble island in the center. The stripped-down décor was typical Airbnb, down to the inspirational posters and small neon signs on the walls. Beyond the island, I glimpsed a living room, a foyer, a front door closing, gray-suited Percy with his back to us just starting to turn, a pizza box in his hands—

"Raise them!" Frankie yells as she sprints across the kitchen.

A flicker in Percy's eyes, no more than a microsecond, as he considered the odds. His gaze shifted to me behind Frankie, my pistol aimed at his center mass. He dropped the pizza box—it landed flat on the tiles at his feet—and raised his hands shoulder-height, either a wince or the start of a grin tugging the edge of his lips.

Frankie skidded to a stop in the living room, her head turning toward something I couldn't see from my angle. "Bro," she said.

I scuttled through the kitchen, never losing my fix on Percy, until I stood beside Frankie. A very pregnant Lenora sat in a plush leather chair in the corner, dressed in a pair of denim shorts and an oversized t-shirt with Super Mario on it. Her eyes were wide, her hands knotted into a ball of anxious fingers over her curving belly. "Oh my God," she hissed. "Who the hell are you?"

As I took a step to the left, the better to keep Lenora and Percy in my view at the same time, I noted that Super Mario was smoking a blunt the size of his forearm, and it took all my self-control not to smile: even if she didn't have Anthony's cheekbones and eyes, her choice of t-shirt marked her as every inch our dead friend's kid, at least before he decided to become a rich prick.

"Long time no see," Frankie said to Percy. "I heard you were dead."

Percy shrugged.

"You mute?" I asked.

"I was dead," Percy said. "Then I got better. Top secret government program, cutting-edge science. They restarted my heart, spared my brain from too much damage. In return, I had to work with them on the most sensitive assignments. Assassinations for hire, coups, that kind of thing."

"Oh shit," I stage-whispered to Frankie. "He's lost his mind."

"Who are you people?" Lenora said, starting to rise from her seat.

"Friends of your parents," I told her. "Kinda. Now sit down for a few minutes, kiddo? Nobody's here to hurt you."

Lenora plopped down again; her legs angled like she was ready to run at any second.

"Oh, I'm kidding, you merry idiots," Percy said. "That night in New Orleans? You didn't check my pulse right, I'm guessing. I was still breathing. What the fuck compels you to kick down my door all these years later?"

"Her," Frankie said, nodding at Lenora. "We know about it all. The pregnancy. The governor. I'm figuring you're the gun for hire, babysit her until they figure something out?"

"You're not wrong," Percy said, stepping around the pizza box, his hands still raised. Aside from the deeper lines on his face and grayer hair, he didn't look much different from the man we'd met in New Orleans—his shoulders powerful beneath his suit jacket, his hands strong enough to crush a skull. Whatever elixir he used to hold back the ravages of time, I wanted some of it.

"She'll be safe," Frankie said. "Someone just wants her out of here."

Percy chuckled. "Let me guess, those FBI guys who think they're being slick, sitting up on the rise in their car?"

"Fucking Feds," Frankie barked, almost laughing.

"They got no op sec," Percy said. "Look, can I lower my hands?"

Frankie nodded. "Careful."

"Who are you?" Lenora asked us again.

"They're friendly," Percy told her before shifting his attention back to Frankie. "I never got to thank you properly for what happened back in New Orleans. It was something catching up to me, and you took away that problem nice and neat, even if your dumb asses didn't get me to a hospital. So, I'm going to repay that favor by being open with you now. You ready?"

We nodded.

"Good, because here it goes." Percy relaxed and leaned against the doorway, his arms crossed over his chest. "I don't know if the FBI told you they were going to break the story or launch an investigation into the governor—"

At the edge of my vision, Lenora twitched and placed a hand on her belly.

"—but you know as well as I do that the Feds are a bunch of predatory assholes, and what they're ultimately looking for here is leverage. They don't care about this girl's well-being." Percy cocked an eyebrow. "You do realize that, right? You didn't fall off the turnip truck yesterday."

"Yeah, we got all that," Frankie said. "You're telling me you care about this girl's welfare? You're her only friend in the world? I guess you were a friend of the family."

"Don't be ridiculous." Percy shook his head. "I have no dog in this fight, aside from what they're paying me. My feelings about the girl or her family, it's immaterial—"

"I love the governor," Lenora called. "We're going to be together."

"Sweetie," Percy snapped at her. "You're a child and the victim of a crime. But I can't let you walk out of here without it destroying my reputation among what I like to melodramatically call 'the shadow community,' which may even put my life at risk. And I'm sorry, you're very sweet, but you're not worth dying for." He shifted back to us: "So, let me ask, why are you doing this? What do they have on you?"

"They said they'd stop chasing us," Frankie replied, lowering her pistol slightly. "Not that I believe them. But we also got ourselves in another sticky situation in the meantime, and we need someone—the FBI, ideally, given all their resources—to bring the hammer down on some bad people."

"Before those bad people bring the hammer down on you," Percy said.

"Yeah," I said. "And we need to do it fast."

"You're the veteran," Percy said to me, and I detected—or thought I detected, at least—a hint of warmth in his voice. "How's life work out for you?"

"Not as great as expected," I said. "But I'm still breathing, at least."

"That's a solid start," Percy said. "That's something to build on, at least. Look, I'm not your friend here, and you know that. Give me the rundown of this shit storm you're in, and maybe we can work all this out. It's better than all of us shooting it out right here. What do you say?"

"Whatever we decide, you're not letting her go?" I asked him. Frankie might have relaxed a notch with him—she'd liked him, way back in the day—but I was still on my guard. Even with his arms over his chest and his weight on the doorway, a guy with his background could draw on you in a fraction of a second.

He shook his head, his shoulders tensing a bit. "No, but we can work something out."

I looked at Lenora, still folded in her chair, still frightened. What if she was my daughter? Would I let her stay in a house with a strange man, carrying an evil man's baby? Would I do it if it meant I'd live?

No.

Maybe it was my veteran's sense of honor or maybe it was because my father hadn't raised an asshole, but I leveled my pistol at Percy's nose and said, "I want you to take out any weapons on you, place them on the floor, and kick them toward me."

"Why don't you come and take them?" Percy asked, smiling.

Because I'm not dumb enough to get within arm's reach of someone who knows what they're doing, I almost said. I was maybe fourteen feet from him in this tiny living room and that wasn't even enough—he'd close the gap before I could react.

"Bro?" Frankie asked, raising her own gun again.

"We're taking her," I said. "It's what we meant to do anyway."

"Right," she said. "Sorry, Percy. Chuck your guns."

"What's going on?" Lenora asked.

Percy stared at us. I could tell he was calculating his odds and coming up with zero: we were two, and too fast. "I'm reaching slowly," he said. Dipping three fingers into his coat, his thumb splayed out, he drew a tiny silver pistol and set it on the floor.

"The ankle one, too," I said.

"I don't have an ankle one," he said, and shrugged. "Just my daily driver."

Lenora stood up, almost shouting: *"What's going on?"*

"Go with them, honey," Percy said, raising his hands again. His smile widened, promising pain, torture, death. "I'll see you soon."

"Lenora," Frankie said, "we were friends with your father. We're here to sort out this situation, okay? We grew up with your dad, we were at your parents' wedding—"

Percy snorted.

"—but we need to go right now. We're not going to harm you," Frankie said.

Lenora wavered on her feet. It could go either way, I thought. And meanwhile all those people out there—the FBI, Monkey Man, Ivan, Dunn, the shooters robbed of their money—were cruising the blazing-hot byways and highways, thinking our names, ready to pull the trigger or throw us in jail or worse. We had to move.

We had to move now.

"Lenora," I said. "Your dad always made me laugh. He was a real jokester, huh?"

The girl tried to smile, her lips wavering and rubbery, but she took a hesitant step toward us. Frankie nodded for her to head through the kitchen and the back door, and when she did so—looking back every few feet—I said, "Move."

Frankie jogged into the kitchen and crouched behind the island; her pistol aimed at Percy. "Move," she said.

I turned and sprinted past her, out the back door and onto the small porch. Lenora stood by the overgrown garden plot, shifting her weight from foot to foot, her face too bloodless in the dying light. Taking a position to the right of the doorframe, I aimed my pistol into the house, sighting onto the dot of Percy's head. He kept smiling, still as a statue. "Move," I called.

Frankie ran out of the house, grabbing Lenora by the hand as she kicked the gate open and ran through. I gave her a few seconds before following. If Percy had a backup piece strapped to his ankle, it probably wasn't effective at this range and angle, but I sprinted through the yard and onto the street.

Sweaty, my knees aching after that short sprint and everything else that had happened today, I unlocked the truck. Frankie shoved Lenora into the backseat before climbing after her. I twisted the engine to life and stomped on the gas. I must have been panting too hard because Frankie slapped a hand on my shoulder and squeezed twice.

"It'll be okay," she said.

"Oh, we're pretty far from 'okay,'" I said, glancing in the rearview mirror. No sign of Percy. What kind of car did he drive? Where was it parked?

"*Au contraire, mon frere,*" Frankie said, shoving the duffel bags of money into the space between her knees and the back of my seat, the better to free up room for her and Lenora. "I think I have a plan."

"You think?" I nearly shouted. "You think?"

"Who are you people?" Lenora wailed.

"We're friendly, it's okay," Frankie told her, before squeezing my shoulder again. "Bro, trust me. But it's definitely going to get even worse before it gets better. Head back toward the FBI guys, but keep driving. Whatever you do, keep driving."

17.

I did as ordered, agents Simmons and Croal gawping at us like dying goldfish as we cruised past, Frankie giving them a queen's delicate wave. At the intersection, I took a right, rolling us downhill toward downtown. I wondered if the FBI would hit their siren and pull us over, or if they'd wait to see what I did next. Croal had struck me as the kind of Fed who'd let a string play out a little.

"What next?" I asked.

"South onto 84." Frankie pulled out her phone and a business card, dialed a number. A man answered, screaming loudly enough for me to hear from the front seat.

"Please tell me what's going on," Lenora said, her gaze darting toward the door latch. Frankie would grab her collar before she could bail out of the truck, but it made me nervous, especially with my sister distracted on the phone.

"Agent Croal," Frankie said, pumping her voice full of cheer. "We're on 10th heading downtown. Just follow along with us. We're taking her someplace familiar, because that Percy guy, he's probably on our tail."

I checked my mirrors and realized Frankie could scratch 'probably' from that last statement: a gray Honda turned fast onto the street behind us, three blocks back but closing fast. Two blocks ahead of us, the traffic light had flicked to red. I drew my pistol and placed it on my thigh, figuring Percy wouldn't shoot into my truck if there was a chance of hitting Lenora. No, he would drift behind us, wait for his opening.

Behind, I mouthed to Frankie, who nodded and glanced back. "The Percy guy's in a gray sedan," she told Croal. "Not doing anything illegal yet."

A block behind Percy's Honda, the FBI agents' sedan took the corner in a screeching cloud of rubber. It must have startled Percy because the Honda wobbled for a moment, but he maintained his speed. Meanwhile, Agent Simmons at the wheel decided subtlety wasn't his thing, pulling close to Percy's bumper.

I took a right before the red light boxed me in. Breaking traffic laws wasn't in my interest, and I didn't want to stop, either.

"When we get to the familiar place, we're going to have a surprise special guest, and you should definitely arrest him." She paused. "I'm not telling you, that's why it's called a 'surprise.' Keep Percy off us until then."

She ended the call and dropped the phone between her thighs.

"You can tell me who the special guest is," I said, "I'd love to know. Also, where are we going?"

"The quarry," she said, "where we had the Great Zombie Bill BBQ. Remember that bit of hilarity? Go there."

"What about the special guest, Frankie?"

"Oh my God, you're no fucking fun, are you?"

"Tell me."

"Dunn. The FBI gets someone big. That's what we want, right?"

"Just as long as we don't get killed," I said, taking a left. The light at the next intersection was green and I sailed through, trailed by the FBI and a very angry contractor. "That quarry is a box. Won't Dunn suspect a trap?"

"Of course. And it's his big, fat ego that'll screw him hard," she said, tapping out a text on her phone. "We always play the players, and if you ever doubt that, remember we barbequed a bunch of millionaires. Where's that grenade?"

"Wherever you put it last."

"Oh." Frankie set the phone aside and felt beneath the rear seats. "Oh yeah, here it is."

"What the hell?" Lenora asked, flinching against her door as Frankie retrieved the explosive. "Again, please, tell me who you are. Besides friends of my parents, whatever that means?"

With the FBI behind us, I should have relaxed a notch. They could take care of Percy and Dunn, right? I had to hand it to Frankie: she had taken one of our biggest threats and flipped them into some of the most powerful pieces on our side of the chess board—provided they didn't arrest us, too.

"My name's Jake, and that's my sister Frankie," I told Lenora, happy to focus on something else for a few moments. "We grew up with your dad. We were super-tight, in fact. Went to his wedding and everything. We heard you were in this situation, and it seemed like something we should take you out of."

"My Dad . . ." Lenora said, trailing off.

Frankie filled the silence. "He was a funny guy," she said. "Always made the best jokes. Couldn't really take them, though."

"He worked with the governor. I don't know on what," Lenora said. "That's how we met. That's how he noticed me."

I was tempted to ask about the nature of Anthony's work, and decided it was maybe better not to know. Did this sick thing with the governor start before Anthony's death? Was that why Anthony was dead in the first place?

I didn't need any more complications today.

"You have any other family?" Frankie asked. "Anthony's sister, your aunt, Maddie, she still around?"

Lenora smiled. "Yeah, Maddie's cool. She lives in Denver. I . . ."

"Listen," Frankie interrupted, and took her hand. I don't think I'd ever seen Frankie touch someone like that who wasn't family. "Listen," she said again, and swallowed.

"What?" Lenora asked.

"If you don't want to keep it, we can help out with that, too," Frankie said.

"Keep it?" Lenora's face tensed in confusion.

"The fetus," Frankie said. "You don't have to keep it."

"I know," Lenora said. "But I want to. I've always wanted a baby."

You're not much beyond a baby yourself, I wanted to say, but kept my mouth shut. This whole situation was a matter for a platoon of child shrinks and cops.

We were lucky with the traffic as we approached downtown, and I bumped onto the onramp to the highway without slowing down, Percy and the FBI close behind me.

"Who'd you text just now?" I asked Frankie as I steered us into the middle lane. Wonder of wonders, the traffic was relatively light for this time of day. Our pursuers fell in behind us, everyone obeying the speed limit like good little citizens.

"Our insurance policy," she said, and winked. "Just let me have this one, okay? I want to see the look on your face."

"What do you do?" Lenora asked me. "You know your guns."

"Well, I work at a gun range," I said. "I used to be a bounty hunter. Soldier, before that."

"I . . ." Frankie started. Her jaw snapped shut with an audible click, and she shifted in her seat. "I sell guns."

"Oh," Lenora said, before turning to look out the rear window. "I wonder if Percy's going to ram us off the road or something? He's a tough guy."

"He won't do anything with the FBI guys there," I assured her, checking the rearview. As if summoned, a pair of black sedans had swept behind Percy's car, and while it was difficult to see inside them at this distance, I glimpsed Croal glancing over his shoulder while chatting on the phone. I guessed they were reinforcements from the local FBI field office, or another group of Feds deputized for this weird pursuit.

Frankie turned to look. "We're build a real convoy," she said. "Good."

I wondered why Frankie was directing me toward a death trap. When we were kids, we'd ride our bikes around the quarry, daring each other to leap into its cold depths. A few years ago, a guns-and-meth dealer named Zombie Bill had stolen two of my AR-15s from my old house and tried to blackmail me, and Frankie had lured him and his crew into the quarry for what he thought was a deal meeting. Instead, Frankie and Monkey Man had blown him up with a rocket launcher before slaughtering his crew and taking over his territory.

It was a kill box, in other words: one route in or out, a lack of cover, lots of elevations where a group of people could stand and rain fire down. She was a great tactician. What the hell was she thinking?

"Frankie," I said. "Tell me more about this plan."

She winked again—God, I wanted to beat her ass sometimes—and said, "Exit's coming up."

She was right. I took it, Percy and the FBI separated from us by a dusty pickup. We were on a two-lane that sliced through brown fields split by lines of scrub, the landscape dotted with trailer parks and the imploded wrecks of farmhouses and gravel lots lined with RVs. Despite all the growth in the valley, this area hadn't changed much since we were kids.

The speed limit dropped to thirty miles an hour, the turnoff for the quarry just ahead. One of the black sedans behind Percy blasted a siren, forcing him to pull onto the shoulder of the road. Was there anyone he could call for backup? A group of Idaho cops loyal to the governor, perhaps?

I guessed not. The governor likely wanted to keep things as quiet as possible.

Percy's car disappeared around a gentle curve in the road. It was just us and the FBI now. I was already scanning the horizon and my mirrors for any sign of Dunn and his men. Most criminals were blithering morons, but a guy like Dunn needed smarts—or at least some animal cunning—to run a successful gang. He would suspect a trap, but Frankie knew that. What the hell was she planning?

The turnoff to the quarry was just ahead, but something was wrong: the old gravel lane slicing through the low hills was gone, replaced by a paved road bracketed by new, shiny fencing. Beyond the chain-link rose the wooden skeletons of new houses, stacks of lumber and rebar, and the yellow claws of construction machines.

Like everything else in the state, our charming little kill box was being revamped into something new.

"Who builds a subdivision on top of a *quarry*?" Frankie yelled.

I slowed.

"Drive," she said, slapping the back of my seat. "Drive, drive, drive. What choice do we have?"

What choice indeed?

18.

I took a right through the construction site's gate. The quarry, once a squarish hole punched deep into the earth, was now a shallow gravel basin lined neatly with concrete pads. On the pads closest to the road, a half-dozen houses stood in various states of construction. The back half of the land was a maze of pallets loaded with drywall, bags of concrete, and piles of lumber in various sizes.

Twenty construction workers saw us barrel through, trailing a cloud of whitish dust, and froze in place—until the FBI cars burst into view, at which point most of them ran for the hills beyond the quarry. They must have thought this was an immigration raid.

"Please God," Lenora said, "just tell me what we're doing."

"Go into the middle," Frankie told me.

"With no cover?" I almost yelled, gripping the wheel hard because the truck was beginning to fishtail on the soft gravel. I was driving too fast in this space, almost sideswiping a house frame on our left.

"Oh yeah, duh, close to something that'll block at least one flank," she said. "I thought that went without saying."

I steered for a row of metal equipment lockers beside a double-wide trailer with barred windows. The phone in Frankie's lap rang, and she answered it with one hand, clutching the grenade in the other. "Hello, agent," she said. "Thanks for following us."

"Put it on speaker," I ordered her.

She rolled her eyes and tapped the right button on the screen. Agent Croal's hoarse voice boomed through the truck: "What the hell is all this?"

"We got the girl," Frankie said, tilting her head to peer through the windshield at the last construction workers disappearing toward the road. "Why don't you come over and get her?"

"What the hell?" Lenora said, her eyes widening.

Frankie ended the call and rolled down her window, the air conditioning beaten back by a wave of heat and dust. "It's okay," she told the girl.

The FBI cars had stopped. Agents Simmons and Croal climbed from their vehicle, their shirtsleeves rolled up, their hands on the pistols holstered to their waists. They marched toward us through the shimmering day, with the confident stride of men who believe in their own righteousness, and I thought how I could have been just like them, maybe, if I'd taken a different path after the military. Too late to think about that now.

Frankie slipped her phone into her pocket, flexed her grip on the grenade, and opened the door a few inches. "When what happens, happens," she said. "You and the girl get out of the car, find some cover. It'll be okay."

"What's going to happen?" I said.

"You won't miss it," she said as she climbed into the sunlight, jutting her chin at something behind me. I turned to look through the windshield. Along the rubble that marked the perimeter of the construction site, a long line of silhouettes had appeared: Dunn's men, all of them holding rifles and shotguns. I recognized Dunn in a purple sport jacket. The Monkey Man stood beside him, the pale lines of his rubber mask reminding me too much of the Grim Reaper's skull.

19.

The FBI men had exited their cars, and a few of the smarter ones had taken cover within the half-finished houses. It was hard to hear what some of them were yelling over the wind and the roar of engines, but I guessed it was some variation on "stop." Meanwhile, Dunn's men spread out, some of them descending into the construction site, disappearing like ghosts into the forest of concrete and lumber. It was hard to tell at this distance, but a few seemed to be dressed in the body armor they'd worn when robbing the shooting contest.

Dunn wasn't a fan of body armor, though. Or taking precautions. He marched toward the middle of the construction site, seemingly unconcerned by the guns pointed at him. Frankie stood by our truck and raised the grenade over her head. Agents Simmons and Croal stood a few yards away, wavering, unsure of the play.

"Gentlemen," Frankie said once Dunn had approached to within a few yards. "If I drop this grenade, the explosion will blow up the truck behind me."

Shit, I thought. I didn't realize I was signing up for a fucking kamikaze mission here, sis.

"Which will kill the girl—who the FBI needs." Frankie nodded at the agents and smiled. "It will also burn up the millions of dollars in cash we have in the back seat, which will mess up all the best-laid plans of Mister Dunn here."

"The fuck," Dunn said.

"You're wanted for questioning," Agent Simmons told him. "Tell your men to stand down."

"No," Dunn said, and smiled. "I don't take orders from this sham of a government."

The Monkey Man strode toward us, his mask's eye holes as black and infinite as space. His hands were empty but if I had to guess, I'd say he had at least two guns and a knife tucked within his gray coveralls.

In the back seat, Lenora moaned in fear.

"Let me tell you what *I* want, since I'm the one holding the explosive device," Frankie said. "Dunn, you're going to go with the FBI guys. Sorry, but you have no leverage here."

The Monkey Man was standing behind Dunn now, ready to back his play. What did he think when he saw Frankie? Did he regret betraying her?

"No," Dunn said, shaking his head. "I always got leverage. After I'm done here, Frankie, I'm going to strip off your skin with barbed wire. I'm going to do you so slow, you won't die for a week. You like the sound of that?"

Croal began to raise his gun. "Dunn, you need—"

"I don't need *shit*," Dunn snapped, and, faster than I would have believed, whipped a pistol from behind his back and fired off two rounds. Agent Croal caught the first one in the forehead and toppled backward. The next nailed Agent Simmons in the throat and he toppled to his knees, gagging, clawing at his throat.

The other FBI agents froze, too afraid of hitting Simmons to fire.

"Come on, girl," I told Lenora, ducking across the front seats and opening the front passenger door in one motion, sliding out onto the gravel. Lenora was already ahead of me, tumbling out the rear door in a shaking heap, her eyes wide and feral.

Dunn swiveled his smoking pistol to Frankie. "That was your big plan?" he said, and grinned. "Have the FBI take me in? Keep the money for yourself?"

"Nope," Frankie said.

The Monkey Man stepped into Dunn's blind spot, drew a small silver pistol from the pocket of his coveralls, and nonchalantly shot his current boss above the left ear.

"That was the plan," Frankie told Dunn as he fell, although the prick was already too dead to hear it.

"Sorry for before," Monkey Man said.

"Don't worry about it," Frankie told him.

Agent Simmons gurgled and his hands fell away from his shredded neck and he collapsed onto his side, slowly, like a deflating balloon animal.

"We better move, I guess." Frankie said, already sprinting around the side of the truck.

The FBI agents screamed and opened fire.

Dunn's men, no doubt salivating at their chance to finally bang it out with the feds, fired back.

20.

I t was like being back in Iraq.

I had one hand on my pistol and the other on Lenora's wrist, holding her back as she tried to buck and run. I wanted to yell that we were safe behind my truck, at least for the next few seconds, but she might not have heard over the crackling roar of long-guns emptying their clips.

Seven FBI guys with shotguns and pistols versus a dozen of Dunn's guys armed with the same assault rifles and armor they'd used to hit the shooting contest—I didn't like the Fed's odds here, but the Feds could also call for reinforcements, airship support, heck, probably a bunker buster if they really needed it.

Monkey Man and Frankie had scrambled around the side of the truck on their hands and knees, crouching beside the front tire. Frankie offered me a Viking's savage smile and a thumbs-up.

It wasn't quite dark enough to slip away while everyone blasted each other.

We'd have to shoot our way out.

Great.

I pointed deeper into the construction site, where the bulldozers and piles of equipment would give us cover, then mimed firing my pistol. Frankie nodded and whispered something into Monkey Man's ear before clapping him on the shoulder.

It was good to see them reunited.

I was getting real McCarthy and Lennon vibes already.

Or maybe Butch and Sundance, because there was a real chance we weren't making it out of here alive.

But then again, we'd bucked the odds today, hadn't we? Might as well give the roulette wheel one more spin.

"Move," Frankie yelled, and we sprinted. I still had my hand on Lenora's back, pressing her into a crouch, trying to shield her as best I could with my body. I had my pistol aimed straight ahead but I was depending on Frankie beside me to nail anyone hostile before they nailed us. Monkey Man was out of my view—I hoped he was protecting our rear.

We reached a stack of equipment lockers. A bullet sparked off its corner as we ducked behind it. Monkey Man ran toward us backwards, firing left-right-left at targets I couldn't quite see. The house frame directly in front of him was on fire, wood and drywall and insulation crackling in an enormous pyre, black smoke smearing the sky.

"Move," Frankie yelled, pointing to a bulldozer maybe twenty yards further away—and pushed me aside, thrusting her pistol too close to my face as she fired one, two, three times. My eardrums pulped, the gun-roar dulled to the rumble of ocean waves, my left eye smarting closed as I spun, raising my own gun to sight on one of Dunn's men collapsing five yards away, Frankie having nailed him three times center-mass.

Lenora's fingers dug into my forearm. I gripped her hand again and ran for the bulldozer. Smoke drifted across the construction site, obscuring my good eye, sandpapering my lungs—and as we charged through it, I almost ran into one of the FBI, a strapping blonde dude in rolled-up shirtsleeves, his left side slick with blood.

I'm a bounty hunter, I wanted to yell. *I was a soldier.*

I doubt any of that would have mattered to him, though. Amidst the chaos and bodies, his eyes had a glassy sheen I recognized from my time in the world's worst sandboxes, when someone's brain tripped into a blood-simple gear, and they started shooting anything that moved.

As he raised his shotgun at us, I shot him in the leg. He tumbled onto one knee and I was on him, smashing my pistol into his jaw twice. He dropped, thrashing and yelling, but I didn't waste time on a knockout blow. Instead, I stuffed my pistol into my waistband and grabbed his shotgun.

Lenora was getting the point now, sprinting ahead of me for the bulldozer's cover. I spotted two of Dunn's guys to our right—shit, the armored ones—and fired, racked, fired the shotgun in their direction. The pellet-storm knocked them back a few feet but wasn't enough to put them down. They raised their rifles, ready to end me as I pulled my useless trigger again—

A flash of red to my left.

My truck barreled into view, Monkey Man behind the wheel not even bothering to brake as he smashed into both men, driving them spine-first into the side of the bulldozer. Wonder of wonders, the airbag didn't deploy upon impact. Monkey Man kicked open the driver's side door and scooted onto the front passenger seat, beckoning for me to take my proper place behind the wheel.

Both men were dead or unconscious, pinned between the truck's bumper and the bulldozer's unforgiving steel. Lenora was already tearing open the rear door as I leapt into the driver's seat, looking around for Frankie—and she was there, too, climbing into the back, the side of her face streaked with blood.

"Thank you," I told Monkey Man.

"Thank your sister," he said, followed by something lost in the hollow bang of a round hitting the truck's side. The rear window shattered. Lenora ducked, screaming, as Frankie spun and fired out the rear at whoever had targeted us.

I threw the truck into the reverse, praying the Monkey Man hadn't tangled the front bumper with the bulldozer. We pulled free, Dunn's men flopping to the gravel. I shifted into gear and spun the wheel and stood on the gas, veering us across the construction site. More shots smashed into our rear, none penetrating. Frankie fired back, yelling something about paying taxes or America or some nihilistic shit—it was hard to tell because my ears were still wrecked.

I hoped the long stone ramp that had once existed at the edge of the quarry was still there, and my hunch paid off—I hit it at unsafe speed, along with the chain-link fence at the top, which crumpled beneath my tires and away. Before I barreled over the rise and onto the fields beyond, I had a last glimpse of the construction site as the battle reached its climax, three of the half-completed houses burning against the darkening sky, a spray of bodies and limbs between the crumpled wrecks of the FBI agents' cars.

Someone must have fired at a tank or three of something flammable, because a sheet of greasy flame exploded from the equipment area, hiding the carnage from our sight. If anything was still alive in that basin, I bet the fireball cooked it to a smoking cinder.

I started looking for a road, so thankful that the bullet storm hadn't punctured my tires. It's all about the small things, especially when your life is absolutely going to shit.

21.

We found Percy twenty minutes later.

We had taken a smaller road, not much more than a lane, that ran perpendicular to the main two-lane. I wanted to work our way to Boise on the quietest route I could find, especially given how people tended to notice a truck riddled with bullets, avoiding the highways in case the cops and whatever was left of the local FBI were too agitated. Percy was walking on the shoulder, his car nowhere in sight, his suit jacket draped over his arm.

I pulled over and opened my driver's door and stepped out, using it as a shield while I pointed my gun at him. "Whatever you have," I yelled to him, "you toss it."

"Oh God." He rolled his eyes, dropped his jacket on the ground, and pulled up his shirt, pirouetting so I could see a lack of weapons shoved in his waistband. Next, he took two fingers and pulled up his pant legs, showing us the empty holster on his left ankle. "I'm unarmed, okay? They took my guns."

"Who?" I asked. In my peripheral vision, Monkey Man had mirrored my action on the passenger side, aiming a revolver at Percy.

"The last FBI car. They pulled me over, took my stuff, even took my fucking *car keys*, then kept driving. Real violation of my civil rights, not that anyone seems to care about those kinds of things these days," he said, chuckling softly. "Okay if I approach?"

"Sure," I said.

Frankie had climbed out the rear, a stack of hundred-dollar bills in her left hand, her pistol in her right. In all the excitement, I'd almost forgotten about our enormous bags of cash. "Bullets tagged some of the money," she said. "It's, like, the world's most expensive confetti."

Just as long as we got enough to pay off Ivan, I wanted to tell her.

"Was that your big plan?" Percy asked, his voice quavering a little. "Get the FBI involved and . . . whatever happened? I heard what sounded like a war."

"You know the secret to being good at business?" Frankie said. "You give people a win-win. I gave the FBI exactly what they wanted: a redneck criminal who was going to do something very bad. And I gave that redneck what he'd always wanted: a chance to bang it out with the Feds. Not my fault if they all killed each other."

"The FBI will come after you," Percy said. "They won't stop until you're dead or thrown into some gulag in El Salvador."

"Nah, I don't think so," Frankie laughed. "The whole thing with Lenora? That seemed like it was totally off-the-books. Whoever authorized it, I bet they look at what happened here, decide the better course is to just go home."

"Which brings us to Lenora," I said.

"What about her?" Percy asked. "Look, I didn't even give the governor's people my real name. If she were to just . . . fall off the map? And I disappeared? I think we could all get clear of this. The governor's assholes gave me the creeps, anyway."

"I figured you'd say something like that." Frankie tossed him the money. "I bet that covers whatever you were making on this job."

He caught the stack in one smooth motion, flicked through it with a dirty thumb, and grinned. "You bet it does," he said. "Listen, can I get a ride?"

"I can hail you an Uber," Monkey Man offered. "But we got no room in there."

Percy sighed. "Fine. Just put a cherry on this shit day, why don't you?"

"Look on the upside," Frankie announced in a cheerleader's bubbly voice. *"You're still alive."*

"Well, when you put it like that." He saluted us with the cash. "We're even now. Don't take this the wrong way, but let's never meet again, okay?"

As we pulled away, I glimpsed him for the last time in the rear mirror, rendered dark against the brightness of the dusty road, the hills fading in the twilight: just another lonely warrior of this world's secret wars, stalking the landscape for either his death or the next big-cash opportunity, whatever came first.

22.

"What now?" Lenora asked us.

"Your sister's in Denver, right?" Frankie said. "I figured I'd drive you down there, help you get set up. You'll get some cash, I'll scrub your trail, make sure nobody from the governor's office thinks about hunting you. Sound good?"

It was full dark now, the lights of Boise glittering in the hazy distance as I bumped us onto the highway again, losing us in the stream of traffic. I texted Janine that we could cancel the emergency, that everything was good—forever, I hoped. Tossing my phone into the gap between the seats, I glanced over at Monkey Man, who stared out the windshield, as blank and silent as a statue. What had Frankie texted to make him come back? Did I dare ask?

I did not. Maybe she'd reminded him of all the good times they'd shared, shipping enough guns around the West to fight a small war.

"Yeah," Lenora said, patting her belly. "This is gonna be the best baby."

I hope so, I thought. The last thing this world needs is another fuckup.

Frankie slapped a hand on my shoulder and squeezed. "We got it. We lost a couple grand, but we're good on Ivan. We're good on throwing a bit to Crazy Bill. We can cover whatever else you need."

I placed my hand on hers. "But are you good?"

"Yeah," she said, the rearview mirror framing her face as a pale oval in the darkness. I thought again about Percy walking alone on an empty farm road, having dodged death once again. I remembered a long-ago night when Frankie, shaky and weak after a doctor yanked a bullet out of her chest, had climbed into a car bound for Mexico, and how I was so convinced it was the last time I'd see her alive. Now I had a growing sense, unbound from any logic, that my sister was invincible, as if shielded by a dark god.

I'd spent so much of my life trying to be a good person.

But after everything today—the shootings and the deaths and the general wreckage—I was more convinced than ever that the world looked after the bad folks. The predators survived, and the weak perished. Or maybe I was being too harsh. A hot shower, a long night's sleep, and I might wake up with my old illusions about righteousness and justice intact. I could tell myself that nothing would ever disturb my peace again.

I hoped so.

But I also wondered who would come after us next.

23.

It's a sad statement on the state of things when someone can blow up a governor on national television and you think: hey, just another day in this wonderful land of ours.

Janine and I were sitting in a buffet restaurant on a Sunday morning, waiting for a couple friends to arrive so we could gorge on pancakes and bacon, when I caught the explosion on the giant screen above the bar. The news chyron said Governor Buddy Hunt's condition was unknown after his SUV detonated outside the statehouse.

Based on the size of the fireball, I assumed the biggest piece they'd find of him would be a scorched toenail.

The crowd around me gasped and muttered and pecked at their phones. I wondered who did it. I hadn't heard from Frankie in a few weeks, but this sort of display was definitely her style—we were a month past the events with Dunn and the FBI, and while we hadn't talked about it, I assumed she was doing her best to clean up the last of the mess, make sure Lenora and her baby got a clean start in Denver.

Janine found my hand, squeezed. Ever since I'd brought home the money, she smiled more, tapped her elbows less.

Funny what paying off all your family's bills will do for everyone's mental health.

"We good?" she asked.

The news cut to a new campus shooting, mortgage rates climbing to new highs, another billionaire running for president.

"Yeah," I said, squeezing back. "We're good. Can't say the same for everyone else, though."

It's what I first learned in Iraq, the lesson slammed home again and again throughout my life: you look out for your family and yourself, because the world's gonna burn regardless.

I didn't know how long our happy ending would last, but I was happy to take it.

ACKNOWLEDGEMENTS

As always, a huge thank you to the crew at **Rock and a Hard Place**; this trilogy wouldn't have been completed if not for their enthusiasm, support, and careful editing attention. I'm also indebted to all my peeps in Idaho who've provided so much help with these books over the years; your stories became grist for this wild, weird mill.

ABOUT THE AUTHOR

Nick Kolakowski is the author of several crime novels, including ***Boise Longpig Hunting Club*** and ***Rattlesnake Rodeo***. His work has been nominated for the Anthony and Derringer awards, and his short story "Scorpions" appeared in *The Best Mystery and Suspense 2024*. His short fiction has appeared in numerous anthologies and magazines, including *Mystery Weekly*, *Shotgun Honey*, **Rock and a Hard Place Press**, and more.

OTHER BOOKS BY NICK KOLAKOWSKI:

The Love & Bullets Hookup Series
A Brutal Bunch of Heartbroken Saps
Slaughterhouse Blues
Main Bad Guy
Hell of a Mess

The Jake Halligan Series (published by Rock and a Hard Place Press)
Boise Longpig Hunting Club
Rattlesnake Rodeo
Righteous Trash

Short Story Collections
Somebody's Trying to Kill Me and Other Stories
Finest Sh*t

Other Novels and Novellas
Absolute Unit
Maxine Unleashes Doomsday
Payback is Forever
Beach Bodies
Groundhog Slay
Madam Tomahawk
Where the Bones Lie